Train in the Vines

OLIVIA'S JOURNEY

Krystal,

And Heaven smiled.
Love truly,

Edith Rose Hart ♡

6.14.22

Train in the Vines
OLIVIA'S JOURNEY

EDITH ROSE HART

Petula Publishing

ISBN: 979-8-9855877-8-4

Edited by Lisa Cain
dropmesomemagic@gmail.com

Printed by Country Pines Printing
11013 Country Pines Rd Shoals, IN 47581
www.countrypinesprinting.com

Headshot Photo by Ryan Arford Photography
2859 W ST Rd 54 Bloomfield, IN 47424
ryan@ryanarfordphotography.com

First printing edition 2022

Published by: Petula Publishing
Contact information:
edithrosehart@gmail.com
Facebook page- Edith Rose Hart

Dedication

This story is dedicated to many, but each holds a special part. To my husband, Dennis, for his never-ending love. My daughters, Lisa and Julie, for believing in the story enough to push me forward, encouraging me each step of the way, and believing in me, even when I didn't believe in myself. To my Iain, Delaney, Reagan, and Adalyn, for inspiring the story within me. To my siblings, Ray, Mary, Margie, Don, Paul, Pat, Gary, and Tom, who not only share parts of my story, but who also have stories of their own. I love you each and every one. Most of all, this story is dedicated to two teenage kids, whom I never truly knew until years after their passing. You tugged at my heart strings as the words fell onto paper, and I can only hope my interpretation is worthy of the young love you shared all those years ago, before you became parents.

To the readers of this story, please know that a small portion of the story is truth, as told to me. However, it is mostly made-up, to make it a good story by pages' end. Read it, enjoy it, and let your heart decide what words are true.

With love truly,

Edith Rose Hart

Contents

Chapter One

Tulip Trestle

AS daylight began to creep into the open screened window, Olivia could hear the sound of the distant train. She rubbed her sky blue eyes and rolled over to soak in the view, just as the train cars started to reach the trestle. With a sigh of comfort, Olivia smiled and snuggled into her blankets. This was just one of the things she loved most about living near one of the highest trestles ever built. Even though she wasn't an early morning riser, she never tired of hearing the early morning train as it passed through her quaint countryside community. The

Tulip trestle had become a popular tourist sight, but to her family, it would always just be home.

As her eyes adjusted to the morning light, and she began to take in the new day, Olivia's gaze wandered out her window to the flower bed that her mom and dad had recently planted. It was full of her favorites, colorful gerber daisies with blooms of pink, orange and yellow. Beyond the daisies were budding rose bushes, and just past the roses, a snowball bush that was loaded down with what, from a distance, looked like actual snowballs. The dogwood trees had recently lost their blooms, which were replaced with fresh green leaves that completely covered the trees, as early summer had finally arrived. The view through the trees was a bit smaller now, but the opening was enough to expose the beauty of a field full of yellow wildflowers in the distance, the train trestle above, and the train cars moving slowly by.

Olivia always wondered what the train engineer must be experiencing, up so high, with all the beautiful countryside below. She wondered what towns he saw, where he traveled to and from, and how many other workers traveled on the train with him each day. She knew the train would travel through all the local towns - Solsberry, Bloomfield, and Newberry for sure, but she wondered exactly how far his travels spread. She had hopes, in all of that wondering, that she would someday get to ride the train herself, to see the view from her own eyes, instead of just imagining while lying on her bed after a long night's sleep.

Olivia realized, as the train chugged across the trestle and toward the next town, that today was the beginning of the week she had been waiting for. Her parents were leaving to go on a cruise the next day, and she and her little sister, Rose, were spending the upcoming week with her Grama Truly and Papa at their home in Newberry. Olivia was especially looking forward to tonight, as her parents had decided to sleep over with them at Grama Truly's and Papa's house to make sure Rose settled in with no problem. They would all be together in one of her favorite places ever. She knew it would be a night of laughter, good food, and most of all, family time. This would be the perfect send-off for her parents the next morning.

Olivia's grandparents had lived in Newberry for only ten years or so, but it seemed to Olivia like they had always been there. As the story was told, they moved there shortly after a family meeting, led by Grama Truly. Grama had insisted that Papa and her daughters, Elise and Dawn, join her for dinner and a "very important chat". The chat ended up coming before they even had a chance to sit down to dinner, and it didn't take long for her to explain what she wanted. She had lost her own mom several years before, after Dawn had moved to college and Elise had moved to Michigan to start a family of her own. Truly found herself an empty nester with nothing but time on her hands, so she spent the next couple years studying her family history, especially that of her parents. Her mom and dad had grown up in Newberry, and as Truly began to learn more and more of their history there, she knew she wanted to live in the small town, where she would feel close to them. So when a home on the south side of town was put on the market, curiosity and excitement got the best of her. Without fully considering what she was doing, she contacted the listing agent and asked to see it. As luck would have it, the agent was able to get her in to see it that day. Once inside, she fell in love with the house. Its strong old structure seemed to hug her as she wandered from room to room. When she stepped outside to explore the property on which the house was built, she knew right away what she needed to do. She immediately felt the pull to call the house her home. Now all she needed was her family's approval, which they - surprisingly - very quickly gave her. Even Papa, with his sweat and love poured into their current home in the woods, with the creek and every bit of nature that he loved, looked at Grama with a smile and told her, "Of course. Whatever you want, Dear." And with that, the decision was made. They all sat down to enjoy what became their last big family dinner together in the house in the woods, knowing that they would have plenty more of the same in the new house in Newberry.

At the time of Grama Truly's heart-felt urge to move to Newberry, "Auntie L, "as Olivia and Rose called her, had lived in Michigan for quite some time. She was happy enough with her current home, but she had been dreaming of the perfect summer home. Although most people in Michigan buy vacation homes "Up North," she chose to buy her second home South. She enjoyed spending the summers close to the ones that she had left behind right after college. She missed her parents, her sister, Dawn, the woods, the creek, and everything about the home on Whippoorwill Lane. It only made sense that she would be the one to buy the house that Grama Truly and Papa were leaving behind, making the move that much easier for them. Every year, after the school year was over, Elise would bring Scott and Lacey Rae to her childhood home, now their home "Down South" for the summer. She would spend this time soaking in the peace and calm of quiet country life, and recording her yoga videos, which had surprisingly become the largest source of her income. Then, at the end of summer, they would all go back to school, where she would teach 4th grade at a public school in her small town in Michigan, and her own kids would move on to their next grades in the same district. It was the best of both worlds for their family.

As Olivia stretched out on her bed, she looked around her room, making sure she hadn't forgotten to pack anything for the upcoming week. She saw her cell phone, plugged in on her nightstand, and made a mental note to grab it last, so it would be fully charged for her trip. She knew she would be texting Scott and Lacey to make plans for the following weekend. She couldn't wait for Friday, when her cousins would finally make the trip from Michigan to stay here for the summer.

Olivia had so much on her mind. She was excited to see her aunt and cousins, but she was equally excited about the week in Newberry. Grama Truly had told her a few weeks back that Papa had fixed up her mom's old bike, along with Aunt L's, and was working on a couple of others he had picked up at a tag sale down the street. This would be the first time that Olivia was old enough to ride around in Newberry alone, and she was especially looking forward to getting out and meeting all the local kids. She had spent a night or two at a time with Grama Truly and Papa, but she had never been allowed to roam the streets on her own. Even with Scott and Lacey, the adults had always been along when they took walks. And now with the bikes? That was a whole new thing, and she couldn't wait to go for a ride and explore the town on her own.

As Olivia looked across her room, she saw Rose was just waking up. She rolled out of bed, feet softly stepping across the room to Rose's side. Hovering over her little sister, she bent down, gave Rose a hug, and softly said, "Today is the day we get to see Grama and Papa!" Rose rubbed her eyes, sat up in bed, and broke out with a giggle. Olivia grabbed Rose's stuffed bear, Fred, and handed him to Rose as she hopped out of bed. Together, they ran down the hall, then down the stairs, toward the smell of freshly fried bacon and sweet french toast.

Mom was multitasking, as usual, talking on the phone with Auntie L as she finished preparing breakfast. Dad hollered out, "Good morning lazy bones!" as he swooped Rose up into his arms. "How is Purple Head Fred this morning?" Rose giggled, "His name is just Fred, Daddy!" "But he is purple!" Daddy replied, as he turned Rose over just in time to land in her chair. As if perfectly timed, Mom sat her breakfast down in front of her. She laughed, then continued her conversation on the phone. "From Evansville, we'll fly to Miami, then to Puerto Rico, where we'll board the ship…Yes, we'll see you at Mom's next weekend. We plan to spend a couple days with you and the kids when we get back. I know you have a busy week, getting everything wrapped up to come home for the summer, but can you check in with Mom now and then to make sure Rose and Olivia are behaving?" She turned around and flashed her eyes at the girls, as if she knew they would push the limits with Grama Truly. With her, the grandkids could get by with anything. "Okay, Sis, I'm going to go now, so we can finish up here and get on our way. Love you!"

After breakfast, they were finally ready to go. Everyone helped load their things into the SUV, then Mom ran through the house one last time, checking for left-on lights, dripping water, or forgotten items. Dad had a good laugh about the whole process, telling Mom that she had checked everything about a hundred times. Mom rolled her eyes at him and smiled as she shut the door, but for good measure, she double checked that it was locked behind her. She may have been an overthinker, but it sure felt good knowing she was leaving the house safe and sound as they headed out for their much-needed time away.

The family piled in their seats, buckled up, and began the drive to Newberry. Tulip Road was a winding country road, lined with little country homes where pets roamed free. There were dogs, chickens, ducks, and sometimes even horses and cows, which would, from time to time, wander out in the road. Micheal drove slowly all the way to the main highway, then turned left toward Bloomfield.

Rose talked nonstop from the moment they left home, and Dawn laughed to herself, wondering how Grama Truly would handle a whole week of it. She decided to give Rose a few tips on how not to drive Grama crazy with the endless chatter, and Olivia rolled her eyes, knowing that Rose just didn't understand how to talk less. Her dad chimed in, telling her it wasn't polite to talk too much, and Rose finally promised to try to keep her stories short. But she added, "Grama says Momma told lots of stories when she was my age. She said it would take her an hour to tell something that happened in five minutes." Dad laughed and said, "Well, you did come by it honestly!"

Chapter Two

Newberry

A FTER a bit more conversation and many more laughs, Olivia and her family reached Bloomfield. Within fifteen more minutes, they were passing over the old truss bridges, which led into the small town of Newberry. It was so pretty this time of year, and Olivia excitedly scanned each street, looking for interesting places to explore on the bike that Papa had waiting for her.

When they pulled into the driveway, Grama was on the porch smiling and waving, just like every time they came to visit. As soon as their dad put the car in park, Rose and Olivia jumped out, running straight into Grama's open arms. They all laughed, hugging and dancing around together. Grama looked down at the girls and said, "I know they say a watched pot never boils, but I couldn't peel my eyes from the drive until you got here!" Olivia and the rest of the kids never understood a lot of Grama's sayings. As she listened, a smile crept across Olivia's face. She knew Scott would be writing this one down if he were here. He had pages of Grama's sayings, and he practiced them, using Grama's southern accent, which was a little more southern than just a normal Hoosier. They say she got her accent from her sister-in-law, Edna, who had come from Mississippi and married Grama's older brother, Arthur, just before Grama was born. Grama was the youngest of nine, and her family had grown to be so large that Olivia hardly knew most of her extended family.

As Olivia's dad and Papa unpacked the car, Grama and Mom caught up on all of life's happenings since their last visit, just a few weeks ago. Once Grama Truly got hugs from the girls and fed them a light lunch, Olivia and Rose went straight to the upstairs bedroom and into the walk-in closet, where they spent most of every visit. For some reason, the closet seemed to be getting a lot smaller to Olivia on each visit, but it still made her feel at home.

All the same games, toys and dress up clothes were there. Olivia realized the dress up shoes were getting much too small now, so she sat Rose down on the stool, pulled off her tennis shoes, and slipped the small white heeled shoes on Rose's little feet. She smiled at how cute Rose looked with her pink painted toes. They dug out all the old hats, dresses, eyeglasses, scarves, and fans. The only thing missing was their cousins, Scott and Lacey Rae. Even though they were getting older, they still loved playing with Rose. It was as though, deep down, they knew how special their time shared here was.

The girls played until they were tired of changing in and out of clothes which, at this point, were scattered all over the bedroom. They each laid down on the old twin-size beds that were once in the old bedroom on Whippoorwill Lane. Olivia stared up at the small license plates that hung on the bedposts, remembering the stories of how they had been on Mom's and Auntie L's bicycles when they were kids. She again had the feeling of deep roots and belonging that made Grama's house feel all the more welcoming with each visit. She sighed a long sigh of happiness and calm.

Olivia must have gotten lost in her thoughts, for as she became aware, she realized her vision had become blurred on her mom's license plate. She blinked hard, and allowed her eyes to drift over to the window seat, which had a perfect view of the lawn and quaint little town of

Newberry. The window seat was framed with shelves on each side and had a large shelf across the top, which held her mom's and Auntie L's high school senior pictures. Old photos, beaded necklaces piled in bowls, hat pins in vases, figurines, books, and some of Great-Grandma Baker's old dishes filled the shelves. Olivia loved looking back at the old pictures of her mom and Auntie L at that age. The picture of her mom sitting next to her bike and drinking a Dr. Pepper was one of her mom's favorite pictures.

Grama Truly had this room remodeled to look just like the old upstairs bedroom on Whippoorwill Lane. Once it was perfect, she moved all the photos and items from there, and organized them exactly as they had been at the old house. From that time on, she continued to add pictures of the grandkids, and Olivia was proud to see pictures of Rose, Scott, Lacey Rae, and herself alongside the others. It reminded her, once again, that she was a part of something bigger...a family with meaningful history.

As they laid on the beds, Rose sank into a deep, comfortable sleep. Olivia laid on her own bed, enjoying the quiet and soaking in the joy this room made her feel. It was then that she noticed the pink flowered box setting next to her bed. Her Grama Truly had told her about the box before. She had made the box for Great Grandma Baker many years ago, and Great Grandma Baker had used it for storing old papers and such. It was the last box of things Grama Truly had taken from Olivia's great-grandma's home, after she passed. Olivia had never looked inside the box, because she thought it was probably personal. Plus, she thought it was more than likely just old people stuff that wouldn't interest her anyway. For some reason though, for a brief moment, Olivia thought to herself that someday she might just look, just to see what treasures the box might hold.

Just then, Olivia's mom opened the door. "I thought you girls were being awfully quiet in here," Mom said. Olivia smiled and said, "I wore Rose out," and they both gave a quiet giggle. "Dinner is ready, and you know how Grama is. She wants to eat early, and she wants us to eat it while it's hot!" Rose opened her eyes and said, "Did Papa cook, or Grama?" Mom said, "Well, it was a joint effort this time, but Papa made your favorite fried potatoes!" That was enough said, and Rose slid off the bed, dress up shoes still on, and went wobbling down the stairs to see her papa.

When Papa was around, he and Rose were "connected at the hip," as Grama would say. Everything he did was special to her. He had been in the Navy as a young man, so Rose developed an obsession with all things with anchors. She even had his Navy picture hanging on her side of the bedroom at home. Her favorite song was "Blue Navy Blue," a song from the early 1960's. The minute Grama played it on her old record player, Rose was hooked. She could not help but sing and dance to the tune every time she heard

Grama play it. She loved the uniform Papa proudly wore when he served his country. She loved him, his truck, his dogs, cats, and she even giggled at his bad manners. Papa could do no wrong in her eyes and everyone knew it. The dinner table was always set, knowing that their seats must be side by side.

After dinner, Olivia helped Grama load the dishwasher, while her mom washed the pots and pans, along with the fancy dishes that Rose had pulled out of the grandkids' cabinet. By evening, the guys were all settled in, watching T.V., so the girls gathered on the front porch, just watching the light posts coming on at the edge of dusk. Grama took her normal spot in the swing and talked with Dawn about what she had planted in the garden just last week. Dawn asked, "Mom, can you recite the poem about Grandma Baker and her garden? Do you remember it?" "Of course, I do. It was called 'Snap of the Bean'. Let me see, it went like this...

When summer came hot and days became long
She'd work in the garden at first break of dawn
She'd dig lots of rows, cover seeds, hoe and rake
Bend over and pick 'til she couldn't stand straight
Okra, green beans, sweet peas in the shell
Potatoes, tomatoes and onions as well
She'd sit in the swing and move to the beat
Of the snap of the bean, in the hot summer heat

Then with the rhythm, she'd break into song
With sweet harmony, as I sang along
I so loved to hear the creek of the swing
The snap of the bean and my momma sing"

After Truly was done, Dawn replied, "Mom, that brings back so many memories. I swear I can still see Grandma working in the garden and breaking beans to can for the winter. Thanks for taking those memories and writing them down. Poetry writing runs through your veins, just like it did in Grandma's, and I have a feeling Elise and I have a little of that in us too."

As the sun finished creeping down over White River, which was just at the edge of town, the quiet settled in. Floating through the air were sounds of laughter from the kids down the street, along with the slamming of screen doors, as they went in for the night. Olivia and Rose were now watching fireflies, light on, then off. Olivia ran to the edge of the sidewalk and caught one for Rose to see up close. Olivia slipped it gently into Rose's hand, and as it lit up, Rose screeched out a small, nervous giggle. The firefly bobbled around on her palm for a moment and then gently lifted off her hand and flew away. Grama Truly said, "Dawn, I'm so proud of the way they play together. And that Olivia, she is quite the little mother." Dawn replied, "I know, Mom. I used to worry about the age difference, but now I'm glad Rose came unexpectedly. With Olivia just turning thirteen, I realize she wouldn't have had any siblings if Rose hadn't surprised us, and since Elise lives in Michigan over half the year, it's not like Scott and Lacey can just drop in anytime. Sometimes a five year old can be quite a handful for her though, so I'm glad Olivia's patient!"

A few quiet moments passed, then Dawn sighed and said, "Well, we'd better get in for the night. Michael and I will have to leave at around 8:00 in the morning. I'll try to make sure and call when I get a chance, but Elise has promised to check in too. She'll call you every night or so, just in case you need anything." Grama Truly shook her head and said, "You know I raised two girls myself, right?" Dawn reached over, rubbed her mom on the shoulder, smiled, and said, "I know, Mom, but I know you're bound to get tired at some point." As they stopped the swing, Dawn noticed the glow in her mom's eyes. It was all the reassurance she needed as they gathered up the girls and headed back in for the night.

The girls bathed and put on fresh pajamas, while Dawn unpacked their clothes and placed them in her old dresser. As they went downstairs and back to the kitchen, they saw Papa and Dad sitting there with Grama's home-made peanut butter cookies and tall glasses of cold milk. Olivia sat down across the table, and Papa grabbed her plate of cookies, sliding it toward himself. "Those cookies look better than mine," he said, and Olivia giggled as she reached over to take his cookies in return. She wondered if he knew he had more cookies on his plate and thought maybe that was his way of showing her that he loved her.

As they sat at the table, enjoying the cookies and milk, Dawn told them all the details she knew about the cruise and promised to buy them souvenirs. She told the girls she'd buy a little extra for them, if she heard they had been especially good for Grama and Papa. They both giggled as their eyes met, then rolled, knowing Grama and Papa would never rat on them for acting up.

𝒧etters

AFTER telling Dad and Papa good night, they settled into their mom and Auntie L's old beds. Grama
came in and gave them both kisses and hugs as she told
them goodnight. Then Mom tucked them in and kissed
them goodnight and said, "Daddy and I will see you in
the morning before we leave for our trip. You have sweet
dreams and go right to sleep, so you can get up early and
see us off." Then, as she pulled the door almost closed,

she said, "Love you more than Grama's apple pie." Rose snuggled up to Fred, rattled on with random thoughts for about five minutes, then dozed off to sleep.

Olivia laid on the soft mattress and gazed around the room. As the light from the moon lit the window seat, the beams flowed onto the floor, across the room and completely lit the pink flowered box that sat neatly beside the bed where Olivia lay. It was almost like a night light was plugged in right over the top of it. Olivia laid there, soaking in the light, when she saw an envelope sticking out of the edge of the box. She reached out toward it, stretching her arm as far as it would reach, her fingers just close enough to grasp the small faded envelope and pull it out from under the firmly placed lid. As Olivia focused her eyes to see the words, she began to think she was dreaming. The envelope simply said, "To my Great-Grandchild." Olivia sat up, tucked her finger under the loosely sealed envelope and slid a letter out from its pocket.

The letter read:

"If you're my Great-Grandchild, and the first to read this, I first want to say I love you. I loved your mom, aunt, and their Momma Truly with all my heart. I didn't get a chance to know you, your siblings or your cousins, and since you are the first to find this note, you must carry the message on to the others. I believe that, before you read this, I will already be in Heaven with your Grandpa Baker, but

I still want you to know who I was. I want you to know your roots, who raised your Grama and who, from all those years past, is still a part of you today. I believe for you to know me, you must know my beginning. I am hoping you have a few days on your hands, because you will need several days to go through the contents in this pink flowered box. I hope it brings you joy to learn who your Great-Grandpa Baker and I were...before we were Great-Grandparents, Grandparents and even parents. We were children once, just like you. Please follow my instructions. I have tied items in bundles and stacked them in a specific order. Only look at each bundle, one item at a time. Each item in each bundle has meaning, and I want you to take all that in before moving on. It will take you days, maybe even a week, but by the time you get to the bottom, you will know me. You will know all about my childhood, my teenage years and my life as a wife and mother. You will also learn of my parents and my one true love. Then, my precious Great-Grandchild, you will have my story to pass on for generations to come. There is no need for you to share your findings right now. Wait until you take this journey... with me and my life, back in time. Do not feel guilty about this secret between you and me, because when you are done, you will have so much to share. Much love to you, your siblings, and your cousins. With all the Love I hold, Great-Grandma Baker."

Olivia trembled with excitement as she sat up on the edge of the bed, slipped the flowered lid from the box, and placed her hand on the first bundle, tied with ribbon and placed neatly on top. The first bundle contained a large stack of letters, dated as early as 1935. Some were faded, with words that were unreadable, like memories that faded with time. But some were clear and told a story of times gone by. Some letters were to and from names of people Olivia had never heard of, but after reading a few, she began to piece together the connections. "Edith Arthur, Raymond Baker…That's Great-Grandma and Great-Grandpa Baker," Olivia whispered to herself. There were funny stories shared in the letters and words that made Olivia feel how deep the love was that they shared.

Some of the letters talked about Raymond being in Mackey, Indiana, where he was staying with a friend and working at a local shop. He and his friend worked across the street from each other and would wave through the window on and off throughout their workday. Edith seemed to keep calling Raymond home in her letters. After a few letters, Olivia read a letter from him that proved that her asking him to come home had finally worked. You could almost feel how badly he missed her. He told her he would be home the following weekend, but this time it would be to stay. He promised to never leave her side again and assured her that if he ever left Newberry again, she would be with him.

Inside this letter was a note Edith had inserted. The writing was shaky, like she had written it when she was older. It said;

"After writing this letter, Raymond came home from Mackey and asked for my hand in marriage. Then on August 17, 1938, he took me to Bloomfield, which was just about 10 miles from Newberry. The local Drug Store there had a jewelry counter, where he held my hand and whispered in my ear, "pick your ring." I chose a small gold band. Dainty but beautiful. It cost only four dollars. Simple, but it was the one that had my heart and fit my finger perfectly. We walked across the street from the drug store, to the Greene County CourtHouse, where we applied for our marriage license. We drove back to Newberry, and late that afternoon, the minister of my church performed our wedding ceremony. Our parents were there, along with a few close family members. Later that evening, we walked the tracks at Newberry. As we walked, he held my hand, lifted it to his lips and kissed the gold ring that he had just bought those few hours before he slipped it on my finger. I wore that ring until it finally had to be cut from my swollen finger, many years after Grandpa Baker had passed."

There were several more letters in the bundle. Some from a man and a lady that wrote to Edith. Sometimes they wrote separate letters and they signed off as simply Mom or Dad. Olivia realized that she was reading the words of her great-great grandparents. She rubbed each letter with her hands and felt the love radiate from the relatives she had never laid eyes on. Their hands touched this paper and their DNA was here, but not only on the paper. Olivia shared that DNA and she felt proud.

Her maternal great-great grandparents owned Arthur's General Store, and Edith worked there almost daily as a teenager. Mixed in with one letter, was a picture of the store. It looked way different from the stores where Olivia's mom shopped for groceries. There were old signs in his store. One was advertising bread, but it looked like the bread it was advertising was the only kind on the shelf. Above the vegetables, a sign read "Fresh Vegetables". Her great-great granddad was in the picture and was holding some fresh fruit that looked bigger than an orange. Olivia wasn't sure, but she thought it might be a grapefruit. The picture was black and white, but Olivia couldn't help but notice his eyes. They looked just like Grama Truly's eyes, from whom Olivia had assumed she, her sister, and cousins had inherited theirs. Olivia also realized, while soaking in the face of her great-great granddad, that Scott resembled him in many ways. She nodded her head, as if to say yes, she could see a definite resemblance. She realized her own eyes, as well as the features of her sister and cousins, held more history than she had ever thought.

As Olivia read the last words, from the last envelope, she felt her eyes getting heavy. She looked at the clock on the nightstand, and it read 3:33. Olivia couldn't believe she had read almost the whole night away! She quickly placed the letters back in a stack, trying to make sure she left them as neatly as she found them. She then tied the ribbon around the fragile envelopes and placed the bundle back in the pink flowered box.

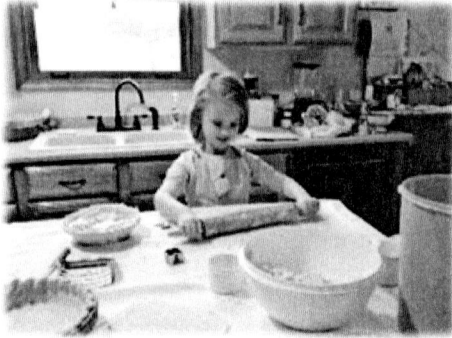

Chapter Four

New Friends in Newberry

THE Sunday morning light came in the windows, in what seemed to be, right after Olivia had closed her eyes to sleep. She could hear her grandma clinking the dishes and pans around downstairs and heard her mom and dad carrying their luggage down the steps. She opened her eyes and realized Rose was standing right next to her, just staring. Olivia jerked from fright. "Rose, you scared me to death!" Rose's eyes were as big as an owl's eyes as she said, "Excuse me! I was just wonderin' why you're still sleepin'! I never get up before you!" Olivia responded without as much as a word. She rolled her eyes, sat on the edge of the bed, and remembered that she was the big sister. Her mom and dad were counting on her over the next week.

She stood, looked at Rose standing there with Fred occupying one hand, and reached for the other as an offering to start their day. They walked down the steps and to the kitchen, where all the adults were drinking coffee and nibbling on warm biscuits slathered in butter and covered in apple butter that had come from the local Amish store. Olivia was glad to see there were enough biscuits left on the stove to cover in the sausage gravy that Grama Truly had made. This was one of her favorite breakfasts at Grama's house, and that was saying a lot!

Rose let loose of Olivia's hand and quickly plopped herself in the chair next to Papa, then just as quickly climbed over into his lap. He handed her the second half of his biscuit and apple butter and she grabbed the spoon from the jar to add just a little extra.

After breakfast, Dawn checked her purse to make sure she had all the paperwork and tickets for their trip in order. They finished going over instructions with Grama and Papa, telling them exactly how to get a hold of them in case of an emergency. "And don't forget Elise is just a phone call away. It would only take her six hours to be here if you need her," Dawn said, as she wrote down the last of the information just in case Grama needed it.

They spent the last few minutes drilling Olivia and Rose on what they could and could not do, how to behave for Grama and Papa, and how to make sure to help them out every chance they could.

Grama told Rose that she was going to need a lot of help making pies while Mom and Dad were on their trip, and Rose's eyes lit up at the thought. She loved wearing Grama's homemade aprons while using the big rolling pin. She sometimes used the small rolling pin that Grama said she used as a child, but the big one, with the green handles on each end, was her favorite. It had belonged to Great-Grandma Baker, and Grama Truly only used it on special occasions, like when the Grandkids came to visit.

After all the chatter between Grama, Dawn, and the girls was done, the time for goodbye had come. Mom and Dad kissed the girls and hugged them like there was no tomorrow. They walked to the car, got in and began to back out of the drive. Olivia sat by Rose on the top step of the front porch as Rose's eyes began to tear up. Olivia scooted close to Rose, snuggled her and Fred, and began telling Rose that they would have so much fun spending time with Grama and Papa.

Olivia waved her hand, and yelled, "Love you, Momma and Daddy!" as if trying to get Rose to chime in. Rose's lips quivered, but she finally let out a shout of goodbyes and I love yous loud enough for the whole town of Newberry to hear. As they backed out of the drive and pulled onto the street, Mom and Dad yelled out their windows, "We love you, too!" then drove away. Olivia watched them until the SUV was plum out of sight and was surprised to find herself struggling a little bit too. She looked down at Rose, with a tear rolling down the side of her face, and took a deep breath.

Papa could see the sadness on the girls' faces, so he took them to the large back lawn where he had his beagles, Lucy, and Abby, in their kennels. He opened the gate and let the girls go in to play, then walked to his workshop and slid open the big sliding door, where the four cats lived at night. The cats came running out one by one and laid at the edge of the kennels, as if teasing the dogs. Olivia and Rose came out from the kennels and locked the gates behind them, so they could play with the four different colored cats. One big fat yellow one was named Henry Walter, and the black and gold calico was named Willow. The two gray and white cats, which were brother and sister, were named Toby and Rain. As the girls played with the smaller cats, Henry laid and watched like a grumpy old man. Henry was rather good at acting grumpy, but the truth was, he loved the little cats. They would follow him through the yard, as he taught them to find bugs, mice and sometimes even birds. They climbed trees together and would hide in the limbs, just waiting for their next prey. Sometimes Papa would sit and watch, then burst out laughing when Henry would jump for a bird, then fall clumsily out of the tree. The bird would fly off and chirp, as if laughing right along with Papa.

The girls looked up at the shop, where Papa had blue-grass music coming from his radio. The music echoed around the inside walls and out into the fresh late spring air. Papa peeked around the corner of the door and rolled out the bike that Olivia had almost forgotten about. It was sky blue with a white basket on the front, and there was a shiny new plate on the front with "Olivia" written in bold black letters. She could hardly hold back the excitement as she jumped on and started down the sidewalk, back and forth from the workshop to the house. Papa wasn't done yet though, so he went back to the shop, where he brought out a smaller lavender bike with a white basket and license plate that read "Rose". It was decked out with a flowered seat and training wheels, and Rose squealed with excitement as Papa laughed out loud at her reaction.

They rode up and down the sidewalk until Grama Truly called out to tell Rose she was ready to make some pies. Rose jumped off her bike and ran to the kitchen door, letting the screen door slam behind her. Olivia thanked Papa for the bikes and asked if she could take a ride on hers around town. Papa said, "I'd say you can, but you should go ask Grama to make sure. You know who's boss around here, right?" Olivia giggled and went inside to ask The Boss.

Grama Truly had a small bag packed with snacks and a bottle of water ready for Olivia and asked her if there was anything else she would like packed to take along. Olivia said, "No thanks, Grama. Thanks for the snack and drink! I'll check back in an hour or so. Love ya!" Then she gave Rose a quick hug and took off out the door. She told Papa goodbye as she piled the snacks, drink, and her cell phone into the basket and took off down the sidewalk at the edge of the lawn.

Grama and Papa's home was on the corner of Sixth and Main, where their property sat at the edge of town. They had downsized to only a couple acres that turned into woods at the edge of the lawn, not far past the garage. Olivia had always spent most of her time in Newberry, right there on her Grandparents' property. Scott, Lacey Rae, and Rose were almost always right by her side, so this was definitely a new adventure.

Olivia rode on the sidewalk and noticed the street didn't have a car in sight. As she rolled up to the corner of Sixth and Main, she looked left and noticed a group of kids in the distance, but they were headed the opposite direction. She decided it wouldn't be cool to follow them, so she looked both ways, rode across Main, and turned, riding in front of the old gas station, where Great-Uncle Andy used to manage years ago. She turned right on Fifth street, and noticed a small café on the right, where several cars were parked. She wondered if Grama and Papa might take Rose and her to eat there at some point during their visit, hoping that if they did, the café would serve breakfast. She loved breakfast at a restaurant. She looked ahead and stayed on Fifth Street, until she reached the small town park. Her mom and Auntie L would some-times bring the kids here to play. But today, there were two smaller kids with their mom. She was pushing the small-est in the swing as the other slid down the slide singing "Little Ducky Duddle, went swimming in a puddle…" to the top of her lungs. Olivia remembered the song and finished singing the second line to herself, as she rode by and waved at them.

Olivia rode several streets to the East, then turned North on Booher street, and coasted until she reached Second. She soon realized she had covered almost that whole side of town. She came to a stop, glanced to the right, and saw the biggest maple tree she had ever seen. Olivia knew that at some point, a beautiful home must have been there. She imagined several children lived there, and that they must have planted that tree many years ago. In front of the tree was a stone wall, which confirmed Ol-ivia's thoughts about it being an old homeplace.

This was the end of Booher street, where the road end-ed. The pavement stopped, and it turned into gravel, just at the green sign that said "Honeysuckle Lane", which was hardly even a lane anymore. It was a mixture of gravel and dirt, and you could tell where car tires had traveled at one time. But the center of the lane was humped up and had short grass and wildflowers growing on it. The lane went down a small hill, up over a set of railroad tracks, then ran into a dead end where a couple of river cabins sat at the edge of White River. Olivia stayed on the blacktop, turning left onto Second street, then noticed an old train car sitting by itself at the inside edge of a small wooded area. It was covered in honeysuckle vines and had a ladder going up one side, and Olivia thought it was the most interesting thing she had ever laid eyes on.

Just as she stopped to look, she saw the group of kids she had seen earlier, but this time they were walking towards her. One girl was wearing overalls that were rolled up just below her knees and had curly light brown hair that fell perfectly around her face. She yelled out, "Hi, are you Truly's granddaughter, Olivia?" Olivia replied, "Yes, how did you know?" As they walked closer, the girl explained that her mom had told her she would be visiting for a week or so. She said, "You can call me Sunshine," then started introducing the rest, one by one. "These are my best friends, Hilda, Farol and Erma." The boys were still kicking a can down the street, as Sunshine called them over. "This is Will, Ray and Bill." They all smiled and mumbled like boys that age do, as they continued to kick the can back and forth to each other. Olivia figured most of them were a year or so older than her, but she thought maybe Farol and Will could be her age. They were all friendly, and Olivia felt lucky to meet so many kids on her first day out.

They began to chat like they were new best friends. The boys were quiet but smiled as they listened to the girls talk about the old train. Olivia parked her bike, then they began to weave through small tree branches and vines to reach the train. They climbed the ladder up the side of the train and sat on top for a while, looking up into the trees that had fresh green leaves. The honeysuckle vines wrapped around some of the trees, covered the old train car, and blossomed out with white flowers that had yellow centers. Their fragrance filled the air and smelled like a lotion Olivia's Grama Truly would wear. Sunshine and her friends told Olivia about the little town of Newberry and what they do in town for fun. Sunshine explained there wasn't much to do, other than ride bikes around town, walk down by the river to play on the sandbar, and sometimes watch the trains go by, which came through a couple times a day.

Olivia's new friends talked about school, Newberry, and summer. Then they asked her about where she came from, so she told them all about her life in the country, near the trestle. She told them about her friends, her school, and her sister Rose. Then she told them about Scott and Lacey Rae and shared the exciting news that they would be coming at the end of the week to spend the summer at the old house on Whippoorwill Lane. They talked until they ran out of things to say, then they climbed down the ladder on the side of the train car and walked back out of the woods.

They had talked for so long that Olivia had lost all sense of time. She looked at her cell phone and told her new friends that she had better be getting back to check in with her Grama Truly. Sunshine said, "We can walk with you, then we will all split up and head home too." Hilda whispered to Sunshine, then Sunshine shook her head yes, smiled, and asked Olivia if she wanted to meet back at the train tomorrow. "We can check out the inside of the train. It's old, but sometimes we pack a lunch and eat inside." Olivia was excited to think they could go inside the old train, so she agreed to meet them for lunch the next day. Olivia told them she would be there at twelve noon tomorrow.

As they slowly walked down the street together, Olivia guided her bike toward home, excited about her newfound friends. As they reached the park, Olivia said goodbye, hopped on her bike and rode back towards Main Street. After crossing, she looked back across the street and the girls yelled, "See you tomorrow!" Then they all walked back down the street and out of sight.

Chapter Five

Children and More Children

AS Olivia rolled up by Papa's shop, she could hear that Papa was listening to the radio. He was trying hard to sing an old song, and Olivia had to laugh as she stepped inside. She knew a lot about Papa, but she had no idea that he absolutely could not sing! He finished off, "I ain't never...seen nobody like you…Whoop whoop, but I love you, I love you just the same." Then they both laughed out loud as he stopped singing and turned the radio off.

Olivia told him all about the ride around town, all the kids she met, and how they were meeting again the next day to eat lunch at the old train. Papa finished sweeping up his shop, then they walked back to the house where Rose had leftover dough and flour scattered across the pie island. Grama's pie island was a counter in the middle of the kitchen where all her pie plates, rolling pins, aprons and recipes were stored. It was the gathering place for all things baked. Everyone gathered there for food and conversation, and it was home to everyone who sat there.

The house smelled like a mixture of baked apples, crust, and spices as Grama pulled the pies from the oven. She sat them on her antique trivets on the counter, then slid the pie dough cookies in the oven. Grama hated to waste anything, so she always made cookies from the leftover dough. She would roll it out, slather it in butter, sugar, and cinnamon, then use cookie cutters to make into cookies. Rose had cut each cookie, one by one, with Grama Truly's antique cookie cutters. After Rose was done with the last of the dough, Olivia gathered up the mess, washed the pie island, and started to wash the dishes. Grama washed Rose up, then gave her a fresh towel to help Olivia dry the dishes and tuck them all away in their place. As Grama moved the pies to the freshly cleaned counter, she said, "I'm going to have to tell your mom and dad how much help you girls are to me, and I had better give you a little cash. No one works here for free!" The girls looked at each other and smiled, not just because Grama was going to pay them, but mainly because they were proud they had helped.

Rose chattered to Olivia, telling her how she helped Grama make the dough, and stirred the ingredients, one by one, into the apples. Then Grama cooked them a little, before letting her use the big metal dipper to dump the apple mixture into the crust. Then she rolled out dough and cut out small apple and leaf shapes to decorate the pies. Olivia made a big deal about how wonderful the pies were, telling Rose, "I could never have done that good, Rose! Papa is going to love your pies. We better take a picture and text it to Mom and Dad, and we'll include Auntie L, Scott and Lacey Rae, too!" Olivia had Rose pose with the baked goods, took a few selfies with her, and sat down to send the text. Auntie L messaged right back and said, "You better save me some of that pie! We will be there Friday, and I will want some when I get there!" She ended the message with several hearts and Rose giggled out loud when Olivia read they would be there Friday.

After dinner was over, Grama sliced the pie and slid the pieces out of the pie plate and onto small dishes. Rose took Papa a piece, along with a glass of cold milk. Papa was sleeping in his recliner but sat right up when Rose told him she had the pie her and Grama had made. He looked at her and said, "Rosie, you sure do make a pretty pie! You and Olivia better eat some too. It'll make your eyes shiny!" Rose giggled and Papa said, "If you don't believe me, just look at Grama! Aren't her eyes shiny?" Rose looked at Grama and replied, "They sure are Papa!" They all laughed and enjoyed the pie that was still a little warm.

The phone rang at twenty past six and Olivia could tell from the excitement in Grama's voice it was her momma. Grama talked for several minutes, telling Dawn how good the girls had been and how much help they were in the kitchen. She finally decided she couldn't hold the girls off any longer. She gave Olivia the phone and got the other cordless out of the kitchen for Rose, so she could talk at the same time. They chatted with both their dad and mom for about twenty minutes, then Mom said, "Well girls, we better get off the phone, but we will see you in about five days. We will be home Saturday, so tell Grama we are going to need some more pie! Tell her I'd sure like some strawberry-rhubarb this time, and don't let Auntie L eat it all!" They giggled, said their I love yous and goodbyes, then hung up the phones.

The girls filled Grama and Papa in, telling them everything their mom had told them about the cruise, then after they ran out of things to tell, Grama sent them upstairs to shower and settle in for the evening. She said, "You girls have had a big day, and it won't hurt for you to shower and brush your teeth early. When you're done, come down and you can watch T.V. until bedtime. As they walked up the steps, Grama sat down with a happy sigh and told Papa she was ready to relax a little herself. Olivia glanced down with a smile and thought to herself how much Rose must have enjoyed the day alone with Grama. She always had a way of making each grandchild feel special and each grandchild thought she was pretty special herself.

After they finished showering, Olivia dried Rose's hair and rubbed her down with lotion, before doing the same for herself. Then they put on fresh pajamas, brushed their teeth, and placed the towels over the edge of the tub. When they went downstairs, Grama had a movie ready to play. Shortly after the movie had started, Rose's eyes began to close, then open, then close again. Grama laughed, and Papa carried her up to bed. Olivia followed, as she saw this as the opportunity to get back into the pink flowered box. She had thought about it on and off all day, just wondering what would be in the next bundle. Would it be more history about her great-grandma and grandpa, or their parents? She could not wait to find out more. She was hoping to find out something mysterious, but she was afraid if it was too exciting, she might not be able to keep the secret to herself for long.

After everything was quiet, Olivia slipped off the edge of her bed and sat on the floor in front of the box. She had the flashlight that Grama always let her keep on the nightstand. It pulled open and sat on the floor like a lantern, so Olivia was able to use both hands to open and look at the second bundle. She slipped the first bundle out, laid it to the side, and pulled the second out to find another stack of papers mixed with pictures.

In this bundle were several pictures of Great-Grandma and Grandpa Baker. But this time, they had children, children, and more children. One picture was of the older four, climbing on a train car that looked similar to the one at the edge of the woods, but newer. In the background of the picture was one of the two Newberry bridges at the edge of town. Olivia always noticed them, coming in and out from the north side of town, but she had never seen one from that view. It was beautiful from the side, with three sets of arches going the whole length of the bridge and the sky in the background. The picture was black and white, and Olivia felt lucky that she got to see the true beauty in color. But she felt a sudden urge to look for that view. She wondered where that picture was taken and how she could find that exact spot.

There were dozens of pictures. Some, Olivia could tell, were her Grama Truly. She could tell, because Grama was the smallest of the nine, and just a baby in all these pictures. There were cute ones with her in an old galvanized tub sitting out in the middle of a grassy area. Olivia assumed it was in their lawn. There were pictures of her in cloth diapers and Olivia noticed the diaper pins holding it on and wondered what a mess that was to keep changed. She knew from Rose that babies go through diapers like crazy.

Olivia thought a few of the pictures looked a lot like her, Rose, Scott and Lacey Rae. Olivia saw pictures of Great Aunt Sadie and realized she could have been her twin. Olivia and Sadie Jo both had long, dark brown hair with natural curls. Sadie "Jo", which was short for Josephine, was five years older than Grama Truly, and their brothers Kent and Andy were between them in age. Olivia tried to remember the nine siblings from oldest to youngest. She named them one by one in her mind. They were Arthur, Annie, Margo, D-Bob, Allan, Sadie, Kent, Andy and Truly." Olivia smiled in disbelief that she actually named all nine.

The first letter in this bundle was dated 1960. Olivia counted the years between the letters of the first bundle and the second. 1935, 45, 55, 1960… Twenty-five years had passed since the earliest letter from the first bundle. This letter was from Great-Grandma Baker, mailed from Ward E, 4th Floor, Robert Long Hospital, in Indianapolis Indiana. It was mailed to Raymond Baker and was addressed to Star Route, Owensburg, Indiana. She wrote about being in the hospital and the doctors having her eyes x-rayed. She said her eyes were better and they had moved her to a different ward. She talked about how badly she was missing Raymond and the kids and said she had mailed Arthur and Edna a letter.

After reading the first letter, Olivia looked at the next. This one told that Great-Grandma had been diagnosed with Optic Neuritis, which caused her to lose her sight for a few weeks. After getting her sight back, she wrote this letter, where she talked about the drive to the hospital after losing her sight. She reflected on how the air was crisp, and the sun was bright, yet all she saw was darkness.

She said, "Raymond described all the autumn beauty as we went, but in my mind were our children at home, my oldest son in Guam, and one daughter expecting our first Grandchild." You could feel the sadness she had felt while she was blind, and Olivia teared up to think about what her Great-Grandma Baker had gone through. The letter described how badly she missed seeing her children and how difficult it was to leave them all behind as she made a trip to the hospital, hoping and praying for the best.

Olivia cried when she was finished with this letter. She thought to herself, "These letters, all these letters, they make it feel so real that I can picture it in my mind. The life my great-grandma lived was hard, yet so full." Olivia realized that her great-grandma was an amazing woman. Through these letters and pictures and all this history from back in time, Olivia began to feel like she had become a part of this history, like she was somehow there, living it with the Baker family. She whispered out loud, "I love you Grandma, and I feel like I know you." She wiped her face, where the tears had run all the way down her cheeks and onto her chin and realized that even her pajama sleeve was wet from wiping away the tears. She sat there a minute, visualizing the family. She wondered about their home and how they must have filled it up with love that never ended.

Olivia thought about how small Grama Truly would have been, less than a year old when these letters were written, and her oldest two siblings, maybe even three, were already married. Olivia remembered how Grama Truly always talked about her siblings being spread twenty years apart and how she grew up with her nephews and nieces all around. She wondered what it would have been like to be an aunt at one year old. "Life was definitely different back then," Olivia thought, as she gently folded the letter and placed it back in the envelope.

The next paper was loose and was a poem Great-Grandma Baker had written in the hospital, after her vision returned. It said,

Raindrops on the windows, gold trees down below
Gray ribbons of sidewalk, people come and go
White uniforms of nurses, kind faces everywhere
Make this a place of beauty, even though the walls are bare

As I look, I am so thankful, to my helper up above
that again I see the faces of the ones I dearly love
May I never, God I pray, forget to thank you every day
For the wonder of the light, since my eyes have back their sight
Edith M. Baker
Nov. 1960

After Olivia finished looking at the last picture in the bundle, she looked at all of them spread out on the floor.

She thought about what a life her Great-Grandma Baker had made and how many lives she was responsible for creating. Nine kids, twenty some grandkids and then it ballooned into so many great and great-great grandkids, that the whole family lost count. Olivia rubbed her eyes at the thought of trying to figure that out, then gathered the pictures, the poem, and the letters back up in a pile. She again stacked and tied the bundle back up and placed them back in the order from which they had come. But this time, she kept out one picture. She took the picture of the train, with the bridge in the background, and slipped it under her cell phone. She decided she would show it to the kids tomorrow and maybe they could help her find where the picture had been taken.

Olivia crawled into her bed, gathered the covers around her face and began to drift off to sleep. She pictured Great-Grandma's blue eyes and a smile with no end, as she was back home with her sight, her kids, and able to watch them grow again. Olivia felt surrounded by love, and thought she was dreaming as Great-Grandma lightly kissed her cheek and whispered, "All's well that ends well."

Chapter Six

View of the Bridge

MONDAY morning came with a summer rain. Olivia awoke with Rose jumping across her and covering her head in the covers. Thunder rolled across the sky, as Grama Truly came into the room and told the story about how God had spilled his potato wagon, which caused the rumbling up above. After a few minutes, Rose peeked her eyes out, and Grama convinced her to come downstairs to sit with Papa while she made breakfast.

Grama made smokies and white rice with milk, sugar, and cinnamon in it. Olivia's mom always called it sweet rice, and Olivia recalled her mom always talking about her Grandma Baker making it for her. She sat there for a minute and realized her mom had known the woman that she had been learning about through the history in the pink flowered box. She wondered if her mom knew all the history, or if it had been stuffed away in the box all these years, with no one really knowing her whole life's story. Then Olivia remembered her dream, and the words, "All's well that ends well," that Grandma had spoken. It was a soft soothing voice in her dream and Olivia wondered if she really sounded like that in real life.

"You're off in another world, Olivia," Grama said, as she sat a small bowl of rice in front of her. "What are you thinking about, honey?" Olivia shook her head and laughed, as she told her grandma she wasn't thinking of anything. She quickly changed the subject, telling Grama that she was supposed to pack a lunch to eat with her friends, down at the old train car, but it was raining. Grama explained that it was a summer rain and would probably clear off by lunchtime.

Grama was right. After breakfast, the sun came out, and a beautiful double rainbow sat in the sky, just past the garden and above the treeline in the backyard. As Grama, Olivia and Rose cleaned up the kitchen and washed the breakfast dishes, they all stopped and gazed at the rainbows and talked about where the end might be. Grama told them a story about the time she was driving with their mom. "We were on our way home from picking up your momma at school and it came a summer rain. It was raining, but the sun was still shining as we drove down a hill. Then there it was. A rainbow landed right on the hood of our car. Your mom and I just looked back and forth at the rainbow, then at each other. We were screaming and laughing hysterically." Then Grama looked at the girls, held their hands and said, "It was then that I realized that I had my treasure right there in front of me. Having your mom and Auntie L was all the riches a mom could ever want. They were my treasure at the end of the rainbow." Olivia smiled as Rose said, "And Grama, because of our momma, we get to be your treasure too!" Grama laughed and replied, "Yes honey, I've been blessed with way more treasure than I've earned, and I thank God every day for that."

Papa went outside and let the cats out, then went in the kennels and placed a leash on each dog. He yelled for the girls, asking if they wanted to take the dogs on a walk. Grama laughed as she heard their feet running through the kitchen and out the door, with the screen door slamming behind them.

The summer rain had come and gone, and the sun quickly dried the grass, sidewalks, and roads, so they walked across Main Street and to the park, where Papa agreed to stop long enough to let Rose play. Olivia sat on the bench and played with Lucy and Abby, until Rose asked her to come push her in the swing. Olivia was glad to spend some time with Rose, so she pushed her on the swing, then the merry-go-round. She helped her up the big slide, then ran around to the bottom and coached her to let loose and slide down. They played for a while, until Papa said they'd better get the dogs back home. Olivia took the leash from Papa and walked ahead with Abby, as Papa helped Rose walk Lucy. Rose was able to walk her with no problem, since Lucy was older, but Abby, still being a playful puppy, was quite a handful. Olivia was good with pets though, and she had no problem holding the leash and keeping Abby at her side.

When they arrived back home, Grama Truly had already packed Olivia a huge lunch. She remembered that Olivia was meeting her friends at the old train car, and said, "I thought you were going to be late, so I went ahead and packed your lunch. I hope you like it!" Olivia hugged her and said, "I love you, Grama," which Grama knew meant "Thank you." It was 11:30, so Olivia rushed to get her bike. She took her phone, along with the picture she had kept aside the night before, and placed them in the bottom of her bicycle basket. Then she carefully put her lunch bag on top and hooked the strap from the lunchbox onto her handlebars just in case it started to fall out of the basket. Rose was busy with Papa, so Olivia told them a quick goodbye, hopped on her bike, and carefully crossed Main.

She turned left as she reached Walnut Street and weaved down several blocks, riding towards Honeysuckle

Lane. When she was about a block away, she saw Sunshine coming to meet up with her. Sunshine waved and said, "Hi, Olivia! I'm hungry, how about you?" Olivia laughed and said, "You can probably have some of mine. Look how much my grandma packed!" Olivia pointed to her basket, got off her bike, and began to walk with Sunshine to the train. All the kids were there with lunches in hand, and the boys led the way, walked up to the train, and climbed the step to the door that led inside. As they entered the train car, the boys reached up, opened the wood shutters, and slid the windows open that were on each side of the car. The light shined in to show an aisle down the middle, with tables and benches on both sides. It was like a restaurant inside a train, and Olivia could not believe her eyes. It was in good shape, and she couldn't tell if the train had always been that way, or if someone had made it their own so they could eat lunch here on beautiful days like this.

Sunshine and Hilda had brought wet dish clothes in baggies and used them to wipe the tables down, so the green laminate tops looked new. They finished wiping the benches, then set out paper plates and napkins. All the kids laid their food out like a pitch-in dinner and Olivia could tell they had done this before. When they finished laying it out, the tables were filled with bologna sandwiches, cut into fourths, along with peanut butter and jelly, and several other types of sandwiches. There were chips, cheese, vegetables, apple slices, grapes, crackers, and several kinds of dips for the veggies and fruit. Olivia was glad her grandma had packed her lunch, because she would have been embarrassed if she had packed it. Her grandma had neatly packed a couple sandwiches cut perfectly from corner to corner, apple slices with caramel dip, chips, celery, and ranch dip.

Everyone shared all they had, and when the girls were done, the boys quickly devoured the rest. Olivia watched as they all chattered about where they wanted to go today. Will suggested going to the sand bar down on the river, while Ray voted to head down to walk the tracks and wait on the train to come by. Sunshine said, "Olivia, what would you like to do most?" Olivia sat there a minute and then told them about the picture of the old train car with the bridge in the background. She said, "I want to see this view, but I don't know where it would have been. She pulled the picture from her pocket, and Ray quickly said, "I know! It was probably taken down by the old train station. Olivia's eyes got big as she hopped up and said, "What are you waiting for? Let's go!"

They all gathered up their lunch bags and sat them outside by Olivia's bike, and then took off walking back towards Main. Off to the right, just a block or so before Main, the boys turned and walked to where an old building stood. It was the old train station. As Olivia looked up, she realized she could see a tiny portion of the bridge. They walked a little past the building and there it was.

The view was just like the one in the picture. Olivia pulled out her cell phone and took several shots of the beautiful old bridge, as if she knew that someday it would be sadly missed by so many. She tried to make sure to get several shots from various directions and told her friends that she was hoping to get the same exact shot that her great-grandma had taken so many years ago. They all pondered at the picture and wondered if it could possibly be the same train they played on every day. They sat on the steps of the old train station until the boys decided they had sat long enough.

As they walked, they talked about what to do next. They decided to go to the sandbar down at the river, so they crossed Main and walked a block before reaching Mulberry Street. Olivia stopped when she saw the street sign, remembering Grama Truly talking about her Grandad and Grandma Arthur living on that same street as they got older. She looked to the left and saw an empty lot and wondered if that was where her great grandparents had lived. She remembered seeing a picture in one of the bundles. The photo had her great grandparents with a little girl, which was Grama Truly as a child. They were sitting on a porch swing, and in the background was a house with gray siding. She stood there for a minute and pictured the house on the lot and knew that must have been the right spot. Olivia looked up and realized some of the kids had disappeared down the hill, but Sunshine and

Hilda had stopped to wait. "I'm sorry, girls!" Olivia said, as she ran to catch up. She explained that she thought that lot might be where her Great-Great Grandparents home was, where they had lived years ago. Sunshine walked up to her and put her arm around Olivia's shoulder and said, "It sure would have been nice to know them, I bet." Olivia wrapped her arm around Sunshine, and Hilda joined right in.

They walked together down the street, until it curved to the right and went down over a hill, opening into a field. Olivia looked across the field and saw the river. The water was as still as glass as the boys were playing on the sandbar. The sandbar blended in with the water, making it appear that the boys were walking on the surface of the water. As they explored, they began picking up small, flat rocks and skipping them across the water one at a time. They would shout, "One! Two! Three!" at each skip the rocks would make. Then the next boy would take a turn...one, two, three, four! Sunshine and Hilda joined in, knowing fully well they could get at least four skips. Eventually all the kids had taken a turn, with Ray winning the most skips (eleven skips total), with the closest other one being Will at eight skips.

As the kids were finishing up, Olivia picked up a couple pretty stones and tucked them away in her pocket. She knew Rose would love to add them to her rock collection, which she kept in her treasure box. Then she looked at her phone and saw it was two-thirty and decided she had better get back home to Rose. She had called Grama Truly earlier, but it had been a while. The others decided it was time to get back home too, so they all walked back to the train, gathered their lunch bags, and broke off in different directions to go back to their own homes. As Olivia rode back toward her Grandparents' home, she looked back over her shoulder and wondered where all the other kids lived. She decided that she would ask that question the next time she had the chance.

Chapter Seven

Hunter's Drive-In

OLIVIA rode up to Papa's garage and heard the familiar country station playing. As she walked toward him, she saw Papa wrestling with the line on his fishing pole. The cats were jumping at the line, and she could tell that Papa was way past finding it funny. She giggled as he finally laid down the pole, looked at her, and said, "I think I'll finish this when the cats are outside." He told Olivia that Great Aunt Sadie was inside, and Olivia took off running toward the house to see her. She hadn't even noticed the silver car sitting right at the edge of the sidewalk. As she walked in the door, she saw Great-Aunt Sadie and ran to give her a hug. Grama was going on and on about Sadie Jo's latest quilt. Each block was shaped like a flower, and each flower was a different fabric. There were lavenders, pinks, yellows, and greens. Every pastel color you could think of. Grama Truly said, "Look Olivia, it's the Grandma's Flower Garden pattern. Your Great-Aunt Sadie made you and Rose both one for your beds at home!" Olivia was so excited and noticed that Rose had already dragged hers into the living room and was snuggled up on the couch watching a movie.

She hugged Great-Aunt Sadie again and thanked her for the beautiful gift. This was a memory that she would hold dear for as long as she lived. Olivia looked at Sadie Jo's salt and pepper hair and recalled how, years ago, it had been the same color as hers. Then she looked at her face and saw herself and how she might look in another fifty years. She knew they, too, had a special bond. Olivia couldn't help but think of the history in the pink box and wondered if it would tell more about Aunt Sadie, Grama Truly, and their siblings. She was eager to learn more about Grama Truly's life, and what it was like to have so many brothers and sisters.

She left Grama and Great-Aunt Sadie, with their hot tea and crafts, and went to the living room to tell Rose about her day. It turned out that Rose also had a lot to say, so Olivia listened for a while, until Rose finally finished her stories. Then Olivia told her all about her friends and what they did that day. She pulled the stones out of her pocket and told Rose how they threw flat stones across the water to make them skip. Rose's eyes twinkled as she listened to Olivia tell the story. Then she rubbed the stones, noticing the different textures and colors on each one. She was excited, knowing what fun her friends must be, and said, "Olivia, I want to meet your friends. They sound fun!" Olivia promised that at some point she would introduce them all and let her spend some time with them.

Another hour or so passed, and Great-Aunt Sadie was ready to head back to Bloomfield, where she had lived for as long as Olivia could recall. She helped Sadie Jo carry out all her stuff and loaded it in the car, as Grama and Sadie Jo said their goodbyes. Sadie opened her car door, slid into her seat, and buckled in. Grama Truly told her she would see her soon. Rose ran up to the window, and Olivia lifted her up to give Great-Aunt Sadie one more kiss for the road. Then Olivia leaned in to hug her, saying, "We love you, Aunt Sadie. See you soon!"

As they all waved goodbye, they walked back to the house and talked about the day. It was then that Grama confessed she had a surprise. "We are all going to meet some of my siblings and family for dinner this evening. You have about an hour and a half to get yourselves cleaned up!" she said, as she pointed to the house. The girls ran back to the house, through the kitchen door, and upstairs to shower and decide what to wear. After drying their hair, Olivia pulled out some comfy jean capris and a cute white and yellow striped t-shirt with a daisy on the pocket. Then she pulled out Rose's dark green capris with a pink t-shirt that was covered in tiny green frogs.

When they were all cleaned up and ready, they piled in the Jeep with Grama and Papa, buckled in, and headed to Bloomfield. As they passed over White River and through the old arched bridges, Grama turned down the radio and said, "I want to tell you girls a story that my momma, who would have been your Great-Grandma Baker, told me about this bridge. She told me that my dad, your great-grandpa, helped build it. She also told me they had a shortage of dump trucks to haul supplies to build the bridge, so he bought an old truck and she drove it for them, hauling gravel and supplies needed to help build it."

Olivia could not believe there was even more about the bridge that she didn't know. She smiled, knowing she had an added memory from Newberry that would be shared for years to come. She was happy that Grama was telling stories about her parents that added to what Olivia had already learned from the bundles in the flowered box. Olivia said, "Grama, that's a cool story! It's a beautiful bridge, isn't it?" Grama agreed, saying, "Yes, it is honey. They don't make them like this anymore."

They arrived just west of Bloomfield and had dinner at the old Hunter's Drive-In, where they gathered with all of Grama's siblings and their spouses. They were all there, except Arthur, who had passed a few years before their mom. His wife, Edna, came with her new husband, whom she married a couple years after Arthur passed. She was still family to all of the siblings. After all, she had been in the family since before Grama Truly was even born. Olivia looked at all of them in wonder of the lives they had lived. She couldn't believe all the things she knew about them already and was still bound to learn, since she had stumbled on to the stories in the pink flowered box. She was quiet as they all chatted, so she could listen and soak in this time together. She knew they weren't able to get everyone together often, so this was a special occasion, and she was happy that she and Rose were in the middle of it.

Some of the other distant cousins were there, and Olivia knew a few, but some she had never met. She noticed they all had common features, and she knew they shared the same DNA that was on the letters she had touched. She knew at some point she would share her story, and boy what a story for all of them to hear! She was excited to learn the rest and share with every member of the family. Her heart was so full, as she had learned at a young age to appreciate her family roots and where she came from.

As dinner was finished, and the chatter was done, Olivia looked at her Grama Truly and saw that special twinkle in those blue eyes. As Grama told her siblings and family goodnight, her voice was familiar. Olivia realized she must have never really listened to Grama Truly's voice that close before, as it was almost the same voice she had heard in her dream. Great-Grandma Baker surely sounded just like her. Her soft voice was soothing, loving, and gentle, and Olivia had a new understanding of what could be passed down. More than features are carried down through a family. Their features, the sound of their voices, expressions, and personalities must all be a part of what families share. Even though everyone is their own person, some of those traits just can't be shaken, and again, Olivia was proud to be a part of this family.

By the time they arrived home, it was almost bedtime, so the girls went up to brush their teeth and change into their PJs. Olivia couldn't help but think of what was in the next bundle, so she tried to hurry Rose up to get her in bed. She picked up Rose's teddy bear and said, "Look Rosie, Purple Head Fred is sleepy and wants to cuddle." Rose giggled, grabbed Fred, and plopped on her bed, but then quickly sat straight up and started to chatter. Grama came in and told them goodnight, and after she left the room, Olivia laid down and pretended to settle in to go to sleep. Rose eventually stopped talking, but then got up, and crawled in bed with Olivia.

Olivia snuggled her as Rose asked, "Do you miss Momma and Daddy?" Olivia answered, "Yes I do Rosie, but they will be home in about four days, so let's just try to enjoy time with Grama and Papa. We will miss them, too, when we have to go back home." Rose got a little teary eyed, but finally snuggled up and drifted off to sleep. Olivia carefully slipped her arm out from under Rose's soft little neck and kissed her on the cheek. She then slid off the bed, grabbed the light, and lifted the lid back off the box that held the next story that Olivia would someday share with her family.

With the first two bundles pulled back out of the box and set aside, Olivia looked at the third bundle. The first item was a young picture of Grama Truly, pregnant, standing beside Great-Grandma Baker. Olivia knew she must have been pregnant with Auntie L in this picture. The next picture was Great-Grandma Baker with Auntie L standing on a chair, doing dishes. She must have been about three years old and her hair was full of curls. You could tell Great-Grandma Baker must have really loved her. The whole stack of pictures was a mixture of the nine siblings and all their kids. All the pictures were labeled on the back, and they included pictures of Great-Great-Aunts Cloris and Corya and Great-Great-Uncle Carl, who were all Great-Grandpa Baker's siblings. Then there were pictures of Great-Great-Aunt Bertha and Great-Great-Uncle Chet, who were Great-Grandma Baker's siblings.

There were even older pictures of Great-Great Grandma and Grandad Arthur, with her brothers, Third-Great

Uncles Oscar, and Lloyd Hart. One picture of the uncles was at a make-shift cabin on the river. It appeared to be made from part of an old bus, but it looked like it worked well, almost like a camper. There were also a few pictures of Great-Great Grandpa and Great-Great Grandma Baker. Then under all the pictures, Olivia found cards and letters from several of them. Through the letters, cards and postcards, Olivia learned several things about the family. She learned that Corya was an artist and lived in Warren, Michigan. Olivia thought for a moment, realizing she had seen a sign for that town, along with the sign for Detroit, close to where Auntie L, Scott and Lacey lived now. She looked at the envelope several times and couldn't believe that their distant family had lived so close to Auntie L and her family's town and wondered how all that had come to be. Cloris had also lived in Michigan for several years, in a town called Pontiac. There were more pictures of the two sisters. They were quite pretty, with bright lipstick and scarves around their hair and sitting in a convertible in one picture.

Letters from Aunt Bertha also had more pictures. She was a farmer's wife and was several years older than Great-Grandma Baker. There were pictures of her with beautiful hand sewn quilts, and it made Olivia realize that Great-Aunt Sadie must have inherited some of her gifts. There were pictures of her, in front of her home, on the outskirts of a small town called Odon. It had a huge barn, set in the curve of a long drive, that wrapped around the barn and disappeared out of sight, on the other side of the barn. The home had a large glassed-in porch on the front, where Olivia pictured Bertha quilting all year round, and Olivia thought it looked like a place that she herself would have loved to spend time. She noticed in one picture that Bertha also had lots of children, and she realized that probably a lot of families were big like that back then. She smiled at the thought of big families, cozy homes, and lots of homemade food, handgoods, and enough love that a soul could never feel lonely.

There was a single piece of paper at the bottom of this bundle that told about a sister named Josephine. Olivia realized this must be the Josephine after whom Aunt Sadie Jo was named. She would have been between Great-Great Aunt Bertha and Great-Grandma Baker, but she passed nine days after birth. Olivia thought about how sad that must have been for her great-great grandparents, and how Great-Grandma missed out on having a playmate and best friend for life. Of course, she had Bertha, but she was quite a bit older. Olivia thought to herself that Josephine and Great-Grandma Baker would have been like her and Rose, and she pictured what the two little girls might have looked like. Then she thought again about how hard life was so far back in time. She looked at Rose, sleeping, and was more thankful for her than she had ever been before.

With that thought, Olivia finished reading the last postcard, stacked the bundle back together, and put it away. She sat on the bed for a few minutes, watched Rose sleeping, and thought about her family. She sat in quiet stillness, wondering what her mom and dad were doing right at that very moment. Then she walked softly across the room and grabbed Fred, along with Rose's pillow. She left Rose on her pillow, put Fred in Rose's arms, then laid next to her, smelling her pillow as she snuggled in close for the night. She went to sleep again, feeling a little changed by her new-found knowledge. She had grown over the past few days, changed from what she found in the contents in the pink flowered box. Love had grown here, and with no one even watching. Olivia was blooming into a beautiful young lady with an abundance of knowledge that was stored within an arm's reach. Seldom in history had a great-grandma had such an unintended influence on a great grandchild, and Heaven smiled.

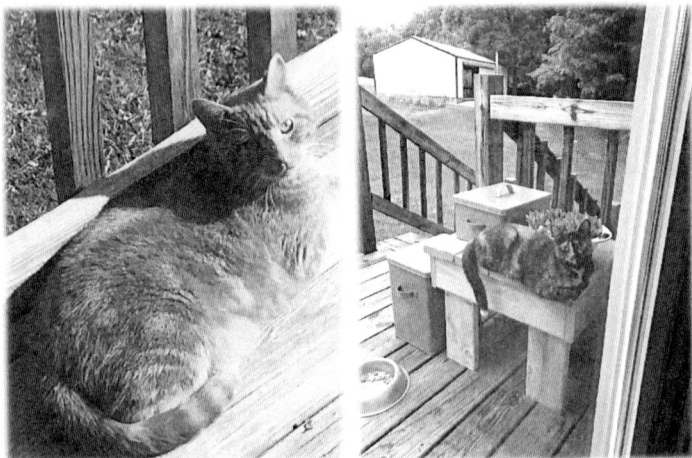

Chapter Eight

Lunch at the Café

THE sun had been shining in the window for a while, and when Olivia looked at the clock it said 9:56. She couldn't remember the last time she had slept that late. She got up, looked out the back window, and saw Grama Truly in the garden. Rose was there as well, holding a garden tool. Olivia thought it might be what Papa called a hoe, and from what she could tell, Rose was "hoeing weeds," as Grama would say. Olivia went to the bathroom, washed her face, and slipped on a pair of shorts and a t-shirt. When she finally made her way outside, Papa said, "We thought you were going to sleep the day away!" Olivia laughed and apologized for sleeping so long. She told them she didn't know what had come over her. Grama Truly told her she must have needed the sleep, explaining that sleep will help a growing body grow, just like good healthy food does.

Rose came running out of the garden and showed Olivia a cucumber. She was proud that she found it and picked it without any help at all. Grama Truly chimed in with a story about how her Grandad Arthur used to pick cucumbers, one right after the other. "Then he would peel them and pour on the salt, and I would eat them as quickly as he would peel them. They were so fresh, straight out of the garden. I loved those days." Olivia had a flash of a picture she had seen in last night's bundle. It was a little girl with long skinny legs and long blonde unbrushed hair. She was standing beside Great-Great Grandad Arthur, who was sitting in an old metal lawn chair. Olivia realized it was Grama Truly, and she had a cucumber in her hand! Olivia looked at Grama and smiled as their eyes met. Then there it was, the twinkle that Olivia always noticed, and amazingly, she felt her eyes twinkle back. Grama Truly told her the sleep must have done her some good, because she looked really rested! Olivia laughed and decided to keep the secret to herself.

They went back inside, and Grama walked to the microwave, pressed the thirty second button, then slid out a plate, and gave Olivia the bacon and waffles that were inside. She told Olivia that sometimes they have a magic microwave that has breakfast ready. All they have to do is heat up. She said, "Everyone is always asking where to buy a microwave like that, but I tell them they quit making them in 1952". Rose laughed and whispered to Olivia, "I think Papa, not the 'Magic Microwave', made the breakfast". Olivia giggled and sat down to eat. Rose kept her company, chattering away without a care in the world, and Olivia was glad that she had forgotten about missing their mom and dad. After Olivia finished eating, she asked Rose to go outside and ride her bike down the sidewalk with her for a bit. Rose jumped up and yelled, "I'll get mine out of the garage!" and went running out the door.

They rode their bikes up and down the sidewalk until Rose was tired, then Olivia told Rose she should probably put her bike back in the garage. Olivia walked into the kitchen where she found Grama Truly enjoying a can of root beer over a fresh glass of ice. Olivia sat down beside her, and Grama asked her if she wanted a glass. Olivia nodded with a giant smile, seeming to say, "Of course!" She jumped up, walked to the cabinet, and pulled out an antique glass with green fancy designs on it. Grama's cabinet was filled with antique glasses, and not a single one was the same as another. There were polka dot glasses, flowered glasses, and striped glasses, and Grama loved each one, remembering exactly where she found each uniquely designed glass throughout her years of antique shopping. Olivia had taken a liking to them herself and always had a hard time picking which one to drink out of.

Olivia wondered if Grama had any plans for the day and decided to ask if it was okay for her to see if her friends were at the train again. Grama told her she could go, but that she should probably come home for a late lunch, maybe around one o'clock or so. Olivia agreed and made sure Rose was in the garage with Papa before she left.

As she got on her bike, she looked both ways, and again, didn't see a car in sight. She crossed Main, passing by the gas station and the café, turned down Walnut, and made a few more turns, making her way to Honeysuckle Lane, then left to the train. It was quiet, so she parked her bike and walked down Honeysuckle Lane until she reached the train tracks, then saw the river in front of her. She had just crossed the tracks when she saw the kids sitting close to the river. She walked down to meet them then turned to the tracks as she heard the train coming. It sounded like it was heading toward Bloomfield, and Olivia wondered what it was carrying in its cars. The kids got up and ran to her, and they all waved to the smiling engineer as the train went by. He pulled the horn, and they held their ears as they cheered. There were several train cars covered in graffiti, and Olivia smiled at the unique designs and creations. She wondered who the artists were, and what the graffiti meant to them. She had always had a love for various forms of art, and she even considered that she might be an artist like her Great-Great Aunt Corya some day. DNA, she thought, works in mysterious ways.

After all the train cars had passed, her friends started walking down the tracks, so she followed along. The girls picked wildflowers, and the boys picked some late wild strawberries that were almost too ripe to eat. The boys decided to spend the afternoon fishing, and that didn't sound like much fun to the girls today. Olivia said, "Hey girls, I've been wanting to go to that café, just across from my Grama's. Would you girls like to meet me and my sister Rose there for lunch? I'll have to ask Grama if Rose can come, but I don't think she'll mind." The girls said that they would love to meet Rose, and they agreed to meet there, as soon as they went home to get money from their moms.

As Olivia reached the house, she saw Rose sitting on the back step. Henry, the cat, had taken a seat next to Rose and was enjoying the attention that she was paying to him, while Willow was busy playing with a flower that Papa had planted in Grama's flower pot. Olivia told Willow that Grama Truly was not going to take that well, as she noticed a couple shredded petals on the porch next to the pot. Olivia picked her up and snuggled for a bit, and Willow forgot about the flowers. She, too, loved the attention that she was getting.

While Rose was still busy, Olivia went inside and asked Grama if she could meet the girls for lunch at the café and take Rose along, shyly adding that they would need some money if they were to go. Grama smiled and said, "I'm so happy that you want to include Rose. I'll let you take her, but I will watch you cross the street, then you can call me when you're ready to come home. I'll come out and watch you come back across the street. Make sure not to cross until I'm there to watch you make it across safely." Grama smiled and pulled a twenty-dollar bill out of her purse, folding it for Olivia to put in her pocket. Olivia promised to bring back the change, then rushed outside to tell Rose she was taking her to meet her friends. Rose was so excited, her smile said it all. Olivia quickly washed her up, then Grama watched as they crossed the street and went inside the café.

As they entered, Olivia saw Sunshine, Erma, Farol and Hilda all sitting at a table with two vacant chairs. Rose shyly smiled, as Olivia helped her settle into the seat between Farol and herself, and the girls immediately started talking with Rose. The shyness quickly disappeared, as they laughed and talked about all the adventures around town. Sunshine said, "Olivia, you said you and Rose will still be here Friday, right? We will all be going to a movie here in town, if you can go. We would love to have Rose come, too!" Rose giggled with excitement, and Olivia replied saying, "Yes, we won't be going home until Sunday, and don't forget, our cousins Scott and Lacey will be here Friday as well! Can they come too?" All the girls were excited and said they couldn't wait to spend the evening with all of them.

The waitress came to take their orders, then they went back to talking. Sunshine asked how old Scott and Lacey were, and Olivia said, "Scott just turned fifteen and Lacey Rae will soon be fourteen". Sunshine said, "They will fit right in! Bill and Ray are both fifteen, and Hilda and I are fourteen!" Farol raised her hand and said, "Guess how old Erma, Will and I are? Yep, thirteen!" Then Olivia laughed, raised her hand, and said, "Me too!" Rose said, "Well, I'm just five, but I bet I'll catch up soon!" They all laughed, and Olivia winked at them and said, "I'm sure you will Rosie! You keep eating all that good food, and you'll catch up real quick!"

Their lunch was soon sitting in front of them, so they ate, as Sunshine and Hilda told them everything about their tradition of the Friday night movies. Hilda explained, "The movie is always outside and displayed on the side of the Masonic Lodge. We can get snacks from the store before it starts." Sunshine added, "I have no idea what's playing, but all of us being together is what makes it fun. Bring a blanket to sit on though, or you will be sitting on dirt!" They talked until they said all there was to say about Friday night's plan, then they paid their tabs and left generous tips on the table for the waitress, who had refilled their drinks for them to take to go. Once outside, they said their goodbyes, and Olivia told them she would meet them back at the train tomorrow around eleven. As the girls walked away, Olivia called her grandma to come out and watch them cross Main Street to come back home.

When they crossed the street, Grama Truly met them on the other side. As Grama listened, Rose chattered non stop for several minutes, telling her about each girl and Friday night's movie. Olivia could tell Rose had so much fun meeting her friends, and she was glad to have her included in Friday night's plans.

They spent the evening in the back lawn, playing with the cats and dogs. Rose carried Willow in the basket of her bicycle, back and forth on the sidewalk, until the cat finally settled in and fell off to sleep. Papa laughed and commented that Rose was the first person ever to wear Willow out. Rose finally took Willow out of the basket, cuddled her for a few minutes, then put her on the cat tree inside the garage. Papa made sure all the cats were inside, put out fresh food and water for the cats and dogs, then closed the garage for the night.

Chapter Nine

The Carpenter

AFTER a late dinner, Olivia took Rose upstairs. They took showers and brushed their teeth, then played in the closet until Grama came in and told them it was time for bed. She hugged them goodnight and turned off the light, and they each snuggled into their beds. In the quiet room, Rose told Olivia she could not wait to go to the movie on Friday night, and how excited she was to tell Mom and Dad about their new friends. Olivia smiled as Rose talked, and as Olivia heard her give a big yawn, she knew Rose had finally given up. Within a few minutes, Rose had closed her eyes and was sound asleep.

Olivia laid there for a minute, wondering about the next bundle, and realized she would have a lot of catching up to do, when she finally got back to writing in her journal. She knew every detail she would write, because everything in the flowered box had stuck in her mind like peanut butter on a jelly sandwich. She also knew that writing about Sunshine and her new friends would come easy. There was so much to say about them. So much that she would probably need a new journal to write it all in! There would be plenty of time for writing once she was back home, anyway. So, after deciding to forget about the journal for now, she slid off the bed and opened the flowered box once again.

Turning on the flashlight, she realized it was growing dim, so she was glad her grandma had placed new batteries in the nightstand drawer, just in case she needed them. Olivia got the batteries, stepped inside the closet, turned on the light, and replaced the old batteries in the flashlight. Then she turned it on, turned off the closet light, and went back to the flowered box, where she again pulled out the bundles that she had already gone through. She was now on the fourth bundle and figured she must be at least halfway through the box. As she gently untied the ribbon on the bundle, she wondered how someone could fit so much information about their life in one little box.

This bundle started off with another of the earliest letters from Edith to Raymond and was dated August 23rd, 1937. He was still in Mackey, and she talked about trying to put dishes in her hope chest but running out of room. Along with this letter was another letter that she wrote years later. The letter said:

"This is the same hope chest that your Grama Truly has now. Your Great Grandpa Baker made this chest in the mid 1930's, from wood used for storing furniture during shipping. It had been shipped from a military base, to a man in Newberry, by the name of Young. Your Great-Grandpa helped him uncrate the furniture, then asked for enough of the lumber to make the chest for me. He brought it to me in the back seat of his dad's old Chevy, and I filled it with hand work I had done, such as embroidered dresser scarves and such. I also filled it with household items, such as dishes, towels, etc... I was real proud of it, and it meant a lot to me. After we were married, I put baby clothes in it for each one of our children. I used it for all nine and we looked forward to each of them with love.

I wanted you to know a little bit more about your Great Grandpa, his talent, and what he meant in my life. He was not only my one true love. He was a talented carpenter. He made your Grama Truly a rocking chair and cradle when she was around seven or eight years old. He gave her the rocking chair early, (just before her birthday), because she was sick and bored. All her siblings had gone to a ball game at the school and, since she was sick, she was home with us alone. She had nothing to do, so he walked out to his woodshop and brought the rocking chair back in. Truly saw him carrying it in the rain, and years later, she told me she has cherished that memory, and still sees it like a movie playing in her mind. She was so proud of the chair, and she sat by the fireplace the rest of that night, content just rocking next to the warmth of the fire."

She went on to say that he worked most of his life as a carpenter. He worked on big construction sites, such as the Indiana University football stadium. He worked up on high beams and had no trouble walking without fear of falling. He worked on bridges, buildings, the stadium, and smaller jobs, but even though he did it for a living, he loved it enough to build himself a workshop and make things for home and family.

After reading this letter, Olivia pictured him working and creating with his own two hands, toiling over each piece of wood in his shop, as he created a piece that a loved one would cherish. Olivia remembered Aunt Sadie and Grama Truly talking about his woodworking shop and how they loved to help him work. They would sit on boards as he sawed them in two, or hold the end of the chalk line as he marked a line with chalk, so he would have a straight line to cut a piece of wood. They loved seeing how the tools worked, loved the smell of sawdust, and just loved that time that they got to spend with him.

Other items Olivia found in this bundle included tax records from when Great Grandpa Baker had worked in the U.S. Naval Ammunition Depot at Crane, a deed from when they had bought their home at Star Route, Owensburg, and a war ration book in his name. Olivia didn't understand some of the legal language, but she knew that years from now, these items might be more interesting to look at.

Olivia had looked at almost everything in the bundle, but the last item was one more letter from her great-grandma. It talked about when Raymond got sick, and how the last four children were still at home when he passed. The kids were ages ten to fifteen, and she was dirt poor by that time. Due to Raymond being sick, she hadn't been able to leave him to work, and God only knows how she survived those years, as she eventually went back to work, kept the kids in school, raised a garden to put food up for each winter, and kept a roof over their head, all at the same time.

You would think this would be overwhelming to a lady who had lost the man she had loved so dearly. But this letter was not just about loss. This letter was about surviving, loving, pulling together, and making the best of the life that was dealt to them. "Raymond was by no means a perfect man," she said in the letter. "But he loved me enough to keep me for a lifetime, and someday, I will be by his side again. But for now, I have four children that need raising, and that will get me through until God calls me home. I have been blessed so much more than most. Even though I've lost my husband, my children fill my life and make me smile. I've come to realize that good hard work never hurts anyone, and it keeps my mind busy to do what needs to be done. Between my work and the older kids being close at hand, the last four children will be loved, raised, and will flourish from the strength acquired by hardship."

When Olivia finished reading the letter, she was amazed that she didn't feel the need to burst out crying. Instead, she felt a sense of triumph in knowing that her roots were strong. The woman that was her great-grandma survived and triumphed in the worst of times. Olivia knew that she shared that same strength and would be able to conquer the world, if needed. Great Grandma Baker was just like Grama Truly had said - the strongest lady she had ever known.

With that proof in hand, Olivia gathered up the contents of the bundle, perfectly stacked, then tied the ribbon and placed all the contents back in the box. She walked to the edge of Rose's bed, leaned down and kissed her cheek, then whispered, "Your great-grandma was quite a woman, Rosie. We have good, strong roots and are so blessed. Someday you will know this whole story, and I cannot wait for you to hear it." Olivia walked to her bed, crawled under the covers, and dreamed of the beautiful woman she had grown to love.

Chapter Ten

Mulberry Street

T HE morning light was shining through the bedroom window when Olivia heard the phone ring.
She glanced at the clock on the nightstand and saw it was
9:01. She had slept in again! As she sat up, Rose came running into the room and said, "Momma and Daddy are on
the phone!" Rose was quickly back out of the room and
running down the stairs. Olivia was right behind her and
couldn't wait to hear her mom's and dad's voices. Grama

gave Rose the phone and had the cordless ready for Olivia. They hung onto every word their mom was saying, hearing the happiness in her voice. She told the girls about the ship, all the places they had visited, and all the different foods they had tried. Although she was excited to tell the girls about all they had been experiencing on the cruise, it was obvious that she was missing her girls as much as they missed her. She told them that she couldn't wait to get back to see them, then added, "I can't wait for you to see what we bought you girls, but I won't tell you now. You will have to wait until we get home!" Rose tried to guess what they had bought, but finally gave up, knowing she had run out of guesses. The excitement of the surprise would give them even more to look forward to.

Dad finally got to talk with them and assured them that he and their mom would be home soon - sometime during the day on Saturday. He listened to Rose chatter about her lavender bike, baking pies with Grama, and getting to join in on lunch with Olivia's new friends in town. Olivia hardly got a word in edgewise, but she was just glad to hear her parents' voices for a bit. She was missing them immensely at this point and could only imagine how Rose was feeling by now. Mom finished the conversation, asking them how they were doing, what else they had done with their time, and reminding them to continue being good for Grama and Papa until they returned home. As they said their goodbyes and hung up the phone, Rose began to cry. Olivia wrapped her arms around her, offering whatever comfort she could, and telling her the week would be over in no time. With the hope of distracting Rose, she reminded her that Auntie L, Lacey Rae and Scott would be there to join them in just two days, and what fun that would be! The thought of adventures with her cousins seemed to do the trick, as Rose's sobs began to fade, and the corners of her mouth began to slowly curve upward in the shape of a slight smile.

After the tears were gone, Grama gathered them in the kitchen for homemade waffles and bacon. Rose sat next to Papa and nestled up against him, as he gave her a waffle slathered in butter and syrup, just as she liked it. Grama told the girls that she had a big day planned and told Olivia to meet her friends early to let them know she was busy for the day. Olivia was a little disappointed that she was going to miss out on a day of fun with her friends, but she couldn't help but wonder what Grama Truly had planned for them. Papa told them to have fun, but warned them that Grama can run around until midnight and still not be tired! Olivia's and Rose's eyes got big as they laughed, knowing fully well that was the truth! After breakfast, Olivia ran upstairs, freshened up, slipped on her clothes for the day, and told Grama Truly she would be back as soon as she could find one of her friends to let them know she would be busy today.

Olivia hopped on her bike and rode across Main, heading for the train, when she saw Sunshine and Ray walking towards her. For a second she thought they were holding hands, but as she got closer, they were just swinging their arms as they walked. She wondered if they both lived somewhere down that street that led out of town. Ray looked up and smiled as Sunshine said, "You're sure out early Olivia!" Olivia told them about her Grama planning the day with her. They talked for a few minutes, then decided that they would meet again for lunch the next day. Ray said, "Let's meet at 11:00 and plan to spend the whole afternoon together! We can go to the river cabins and fish off the bank, then take a walk down the tracks and see if any trains come by." Sunshine and Olivia agreed that Ray's plans sounded like a great way to spend an afternoon. Once the plans were set, Olivia told them she had to get back home, so she and Rose could spend the rest of the day with Grama Truly. She said goodbye with the promise that she'd see them tomorrow with more of her grandma's tasty food for lunch, and with that, they said goodbye. As Olivia headed toward home, Sunshine and Ray turned back down the street to head to the train.

Olivia arrived back at the house as Grama was packing her Jeep with a picnic basket, table cloth, and blanket. Rose came out of the house with a small basket filled with fresh cookies in one hand, and a jug full of fresh lemonade in her other hand. It was about all she could carry, so Olivia ran over to lend a hand and help her carry it the rest of the way to the Jeep. They finished loading what

Grama had packed, told Papa goodbye, and headed down the back street just north of their backyard. Olivia looked up and noticed that this was Mulberry Street. She couldn't believe that she hadn't realized that this street was right out Grama Truly's back door. Grama drove several blocks down and stopped at the open lot that had interested Olivia just a few days before.

Grama Truly began to tell the girls that this was the last place her grandparents had lived, and that the Arthur's General Store had set just at the back of the house, facing Main Street. She told them that today she wanted to share some of the memories her mom had shared with her, and she also planned to share some of her own memories with them. "I know you probably won't remember all I show you, but it will be good for you to know some family history. I also just wanted to spend the day out with you girls!" Grama said. She opened her car door and both girls followed. As she got out of the jeep, she walked toward a rose bush full of beautiful white roses. Olivia took a deep breath as she smelled the amazing fragrance that came from the bush. Then she turned to Rose and told her to smell. Grama walked to the second bush that had the brightest pink roses Olivia had ever seen. Grama told them, "I don't know who actually owns this property now, but these roses have been here for many, many years. The owner of the property has a local man mow during the summer, and he asked if I would mind tending the rose bushes, so I have my grandma's fresh roses all summer long." She snipped a few of the most beautiful roses off, handed one to each girl and put the rest in an old mason jar from the back of her jeep. She told Rose that she must have been named after the pink roses, because she was as colorful as they were. Rose posed with her favorite cute-face pose, and Olivia laughed and rolled her eyes. With playful hugging and giggling, they made their way back to the jeep, then hopped in to see where they were headed next.

As they turned back onto Main Street, Grama pulled over on the lot where the old store would have been. She told them a story her mom had told her. She said, "Your great-grandma used to tell me about her and her dad. He had a wagon that they drove to area farms. He sold goods and groceries to families out of the wagon. Sometimes the families would trade homegrown vegetables, fruits, eggs and such to pay for what they needed in exchange. They called the wagon a 'peddle wagon', which meant it was a wagon used for selling goods." She told them that Great Grandma also worked in the store as a teenager, helping her dad whenever he needed. On Friday nights, the town would have movies on the side of the Masonic Lodge, which was right next door to the store. Everyone would stop in for snacks and drinks before the movie, so Mom would help him during the busy time, then go back out with her friends once the movie started. "Things were so

different back then, but I bet it was a good life they lived."
By this time, both Olivia and Rose were hanging on every word Grama Truly was saying, and Olivia realized the tradition of having the movie on Friday night was still carried on to this day. Grama Truly could tell they were taking in everything she said, so she took advantage of that and told them all she could tell them in a day.

After telling all about her grandad's store, Grama Truly pointed across the street and told the girls that their other Great-Great Grandpa Baker owned a blacksmith shop there. Olivia was intrigued that both sets of grandparents owned businesses right across from each other. Grama explained that part of the old blacksmith shop still remained, and that the front of the building had been added on to several times throughout the years. They drove across to the building, and followed the road behind it, as she explained that their Great Grandpa Baker lived just at the foot of the hill when he was growing up. She explained, "All of the old houses are gone now, but I'm going to show you where they were, just so you know".

Chapter Eleven

Memories with Grama Truly

AS they turned south, Olivia remembered that was exactly where she had met with Sunshine and Ray just this morning. She started to wonder what they were doing today, then realized she was only half listening to her grandma. Olivia's mind snapped back, just as her Grama was pulling over in front of the church that Olivia passed by each day, on her way to the train. Her grandma smiled and said, "I want to tell you girls a story your Great Grandma Edie told me years ago. It's probably my favorite story she ever told me." As Truly got out of the jeep, she said, "My mom told me she used to go to the movies with Dad every week, because they were best friends. Then one Friday night, he asked another girl to go with him. It was the first time he didn't go with her. Mom was wearing a new pair of shoes that evening, and after the movies, it began to rain. Mom and her parents lived just outside the edge of town at that time, and she had to walk home. She came to this church and stood in the entry, hoping the rain would stop, so she didn't ruin her new shoes. As she stood there, she saw my dad walking the other girl home. Then, a few minutes later, he came back. He had seen her in the church and stopped to talk with her. She told him she didn't want to ruin her new shoes, so he put her on his back and carried her all the way home. From that day forward, they were boyfriend and girlfriend." Olivia thought about her great-grandma and grandpa, and she began to picture them walking in the rain that night, right there on that street. The thought of such a sweet beginning brought a smile to her face, and to her heart.

After some time imagining the story of her grandparents on that rainy evening, Olivia, Grama Truly and Rose got back in the car. They turned left on the road that led out of town, and as she drove, Grama went on to say that her mom and grandparents went to that church and that her mom and Grandad Arthur would sometimes sing together there. Then she said, "We will go past the place my mom lived as a teenager, where my dad carried her after the movies that night. Then I'll take you where her old farm used to be, when she was younger."

They had driven just a few blocks out of town when Grama Truly pulled into an old drive, where a newer barn now stood, and started talking about the house that once sat there. She said, "I actually remember the house that sat here. By the time I was a kid, the house was old and run down, and it was used to store hay. But even then, you could tell it was a beautiful home years before. It was white, and I remember an octagon window on the side facing the road. I always wondered what room it might have been...the living room or one of the bedrooms, maybe? Every time we would come to Newberry, Mom would tell stories about when she lived here. She told me lots of stories, like the movie night, with her new shoes and Dad in the rain, and those stories took me back in time, just like I was there. I could see her with her light brown hair laying in curls. Sometimes I pictured her in flowing dresses, or simply in a pair of overalls. No matter how I pictured her, she was always a beauty, just like in her pictures. I have to wonder if the octagon window was in the room where she slept, and if the moon shone in on her face just to get a glimpse of her beauty itself." Rose said, "She sounds like a princess, Grama!" Grama laughed and answered back, "She was a princess, Rosie! She just wore her crown in curls." Olivia and Rose looked at each other with a twinkle in their eyes, knowing it must have been true. Grama Edie must have been a princess, at least for the town of Newberry.

They continued down the road, ending up at the end of a long lane. Grama stopped and said, "This is where Uncle Andy says my Grandma and Grandad Arthur's farm was. My mom was pretty young when she lived here, and before that, they lived in Newark, where Grandad had owned his first store. I'm not really sure of any of the details. I wish I had asked Mom a few more questions. That history is just gone, with no one here to tell the whole story. Some of my siblings know bits and pieces, but I guess that's what happens with time. You have to grasp onto every story, and try to keep the history alive."

Grama Truly got out of her car and motioned the girls out. She said, "Grab the mason jar out of the back and we will add these flowers." She reached up to the bank, on the side of the road, and snipped a group of orange flowers that were mixed in with weeds. Then, she added them to the roses in the jar, arranging them into a perfect bouquet, like Olivia had seen them do at the flower shop when her dad bought her mom flowers for Valentine's Day. When she was done gathering all she wanted, she told the girls that the flowers were called Tiger Lilies. "Your Grandma Edie would stop around this area to pick these flowers each time we drove by, so I always do the same." Truly sat the jar in the back of the car, but this time, she put it in a basket and added some water from the bottle she had been drinking. She stuffed a towel around it, making sure it was secure, then shut the rear door and started out again.

As they got back in the car, they all rolled down their windows and listened to the old songs that Dawn had downloaded on Grama Truly's phone. All of Grama's favorites were there, and they had become Olivia's and Rose's favorites over time also. There were songs from several decades, but Grama loved them all. Blue Navy Blue, Que Sera Sera, What a Wonderful World, Crimson and Clover, then a couple of Beatles songs, Hey Jude and Paperback Writer. They moved on to the seventies, and listened to Grama Truly's senior class song. It was played at her Senior prom and was titled "Colour my World," by the group Chicago.

They listened and sang all the way from the farm to highway 231. They turned onto highway 58 and passed by the road that led to Scotland, driving until they reached Doans. Truly turned on Whippoorwill Lane, telling the girls that she was going to stop by the old homeplace, turn on the air conditioning, and make sure the house was ready for Auntie L to come at the end of the week.

She drove down the gravel, past the old Martindale property, then on around the corner, until they saw the familiar home, where Auntie L, Scott and Lacey Rae would soon be enjoying the summer months. Grama Truly was so excited to spend time with them again. She loved telling people how Elise lived a pretty simple life as a teacher, but she had excelled with recording and promoting her yoga videos. She had recorded her first video right there at the old house and was surprised when it gained traction, started selling, and became a strong source of revenue. She always said the surrounding nature was what made her videos so interesting to her clients. "Nothing calms a soul like the sound of birds singing, wind chimes moving slowly, and dried dandelion seeds blowing in the wind."

After Grama finished in the house, they pulled out onto the highway and drove slowly past the next homestead up the road. She told the girls the house was gone, but she had lived on this property as a newborn, then moved to another house up the road when she was four. She told them that most of the older kids had grown up here and they always referred to it as the basement house, which sat on the hill, then later, the blue house, which sat at the bottom of the property. She talked about the memories there until they made their next stop.

They drove to Kentucky Ridge Church, pulled into the gravel drive, and to the gravesite where Great Grandma and Grandpa Baker were laid to rest. Olivia swallowed hard, trying not to cry, when she realized where they were. She put her hand over her heart as she thought about the letters in the bundles from the pink flowered box. She opened the door of the Jeep, fixing her eyes on the names on the stone. She walked to it and knelt down, doing all she could to not let her grandma see the tear rolling down the side of her cheek.

Truly opened the back of the jeep and pulled out the fresh flowers they had picked along the way. She carried them to the grave and handed them to the girls, asking them to place them in the vases that were attached to the gravestone. The stone was a simple one, but just like Grandma Edie's wedding band, it served the purpose. As Olivia, Rose and Grama Truly looked at the stone, they admired the oval picture placed in its center. The stone read, "Raymond and Edith Baker" and in the picture, they were sitting on the front bumper of an old Model A Ford. To this day, the photo is still the most cherished family picture. Even though it was just a black and white photo, Edith's beauty stood out, as her hair laid in curls, and her eyes glittered in the sunlight. Olivia could see Auntie L's face in Edith's, and also, her own mom's, and even Grama Truly's face was mixed in Great Grandma's face. Raymond was quite a handsome man himself, and you could tell he was proud to have her as his girl. Both were in the prime of their lives in this photo, and it was perfect.

As Olivia read the dates, she realized that he was only fifty-two years old when he had passed, and for a minute, she fought back the tears again. She looked out over the graveyard, then looked back at the stone, this time counting the years Grandma Edie had on earth. Eighty four. She had lived over thirty years past him, finishing out the life they should have had together. Grama Truly wiped a tear from her eye, then took a deep breath. She looked at the girls and said, "Girls, right here lies the strongest, bravest woman I've ever known. I know today my mom and dad are smiling down together, knowing what a beautiful family they created together. Olivia hugged Grama Truly close for a minute, knowing that she had no idea that Olivia had been learning the whole story from the bundles in the box this week, and exactly how special this moment was to her.

When they were done paying their respects, Grama walked back to the car with the girls not far behind. They got back in the Jeep again, then drove around the graveyard, as Olivia read the names on the stones of so many lives gone by. Then Truly pulled back to the front of the church, opened her door, and hurried out to ring the large bell that hung just outside the front door. Rose cackled as Grama rang the bell several times, before they could even get to her. Once they got to her, Grama lifted Rose up to reach the rope, then let her full weight down on it, to get it to ring out for the people in the surrounding homes to hear. Olivia took her turn and rang it several times, before tiring from the weight of the bell. They all laughed as they collapsed in a pile together on the church steps. The girls snuggled up on each side of Grama Truly, knowing fully well that she had a story to share about the bell.

Grama said, "When I was a kid, we would ring this bell at the beginning of church each Sunday. Then on New Year's Eve, we would have a big party here at the church. At the stroke of midnight, we would ring the bell for the amount of years. So, in 1969, we rang it 69 times! We would all form a line and take turns, shouting the number as the bell rang. We loved to ring this old bell and never tired of it." They sat there for a while, as Grama talked about one of the old men that used to come to church here. She said, "He wore overalls every Sunday, but he always had a flower in his pocket, along with Juicy Fruit or Wrigley's Spearmint gum. All of us kids knew to see him after church, because the gum never seemed to run out. Never one time did I ask for gum and not get it. I guess that's why I always try to have goodies for kids. Sweet candy or gum is a must when kids are around!"

Chapter Twelve

Childhood Home

A S they drove to the next stop, the girls' excitement grew. Grama pulled into the driveway of her childhood home. Over the years, Grama had pointed the home out several times as the place she had grown up. But they had never driven up into the driveway. She told them the house was up for sale, and she was friends with the owners, who had agreed to let them spend a few hours there. She pulled a key from her pocket and opened the front door to the home that had a large part of her life's memories stored inside.

They went inside the living room and admired the old fireplace that had been restored to the original brick. Truly remembered the brick from when she was a child, then remembered during her teenage years, her brother Kent had covered it in fieldstone. It was beautiful both ways, but seeing the brick brought back memories of those earlier days, when her dad was there with them. It was in front of this fireplace that she sat, in the rocking chair her dad had made. Olivia hugged her as she looked a little teary eyed, then Grama smiled and began to walk through the doorway that led to the next open room.

They walked through each room as Grama Truly told them every detail she could remember. Then, as they reached the kitchen, Grama Truly rubbed the concrete of an old arched opening, which went straight into the kitchen. Olivia and Rose watched, as they could tell Grama Truly had fond memories of her childhood there. Olivia looked through the arch and into the kitchen, where the table was. She pictured Grama Edie, Papa Baker, and all of the kids gathered there at the table. How many meals they must have shared here. Olivia could almost hear the voices of all the kids as the food was passed bowl by bowl around the table.

As they walked into the kitchen, Grama gasped as she noticed the table was set for what looked like a dozen people, then noticed a note from the owners. They explained that she didn't need to carry in her picnic basket, because they had prepared a meal for them and had left it in the oven, and microwave. The note finished by saying, "We set the table for several extra, because we think you will probably have visitors soon."

They giggled with laughter after reading the note, and just as they looked in the oven, they heard a knock on the front door. The girls ran through the house, and Truly thought back to that old familiar sound of children's feet running down the hallway. As the girls reached the door, they yelled out, "It's Aunt Sadie Jo!" Truly was so excited, she grabbed and hugged Sadie Jo and said, "How did you know we would be here?" Sadie explained that their friend had called her and let her in on the secret, so she shared it with the other siblings, who walked in behind her one by one. Aunt Annie and Margo walked in behind Aunt Sadie Jo, then came Uncles D-Bob, Allan, Kent and Andy.

They went to the kitchen, pulled out the food, and enjoyed the meal together, as each sibling talked of older days gone by. Olivia and Rose took in every detail, then after lunch, they wrote a note to the owners, thanking them for their thoughtfulness and the delicious meal. Each sibling signed it along with Olivia and Rose, then Truly added a P.S. at the end, promising them a few pies in the near future.

When they finished cleaning up after the meal, they explored the whole house, sat on the beds in their old rooms, and ended up on the front lawn, some in lawn chairs, and some on a couple old blankets from their childhood, which Sadie Jo had brought from her home. As D-Bob, Allan, and Kent sang and played their guitars, Truly sang along. The aunts picked clover flowers that were scattered over the whole lawn and showed Olivia and Rose how to tie them together to make chain bracelets, necklaces, and even crowns to adorn their hair.

After they sang all the songs they could remember, they walked behind the house to the old woodshop where Grandpa Baker had spent his spare time. His tools were gone, and it sat empty now. Olivia wondered if it had been empty all these years, or if it was just empty because the house was up for sale. Sadie Jo climbed up on a ladder that sat below the attic, and climbed up in. She was gone for a few minutes, as the boys talked about some of the memories gathered there, then Sadie Jo peaked out the attic door, and said, "Guys, look what I found." She handed down a pair of old striped overalls that their dad had worn all those years ago. She cried as she hugged them, then she smiled and said, "He knew I'd be back to get these".

After drying the tears, they walked around the lawn. Truly showed the girls the trees they used to climb with their brothers, and the older uncles pointed out where the gardens had once been planted, remembering the rows and rows of vegetables to which they tended all those years ago.

They told stories of rubber band baseball, which was the same as baseball, but they used a homemade ball made out of rubber bands. They recalled how they would play out in the field, and the ball would go forever if they didn't manage to catch it. They told about the joys of talking on phones that were attached to party lines, which were shared with the neighbors, and they laughed when remembering the old woman next door and how she would listen in on their phone conversations. They talked about the man and his wife who used to live across the street, and about how beautiful his pastel chalk drawings were.

It was late evening by the time Truly and her siblings had stopped telling the girls stories. Allan finished off the evening playing his trumpet next to the well, which he pointed into the opening, making it echo throughout the countryside. As he played "Look Down That Lonesome Road," Truly recalled how neighbors would comment on how lovely the sound was, and hearing it again warmed her heart. She hoped some of the old folks were still around to hear.

They said their goodbyes, loaded up in their cars, and each turned the direction of their own separate homes. Truly followed Aunt Sadie until she turned to head back to her home in Bloomfield, then she took the country road back toward Newberry. The ride back to Grama Truly's was mostly quiet, except for Grama softly singing a few old gospel songs she used to sing with her mom, and that she had sung just a few short hours ago with her brothers. Olivia and Rose both sang what they remembered, and by the time they arrived home, Olivia was pretty sure she would remember the songs for the rest of her life.

After reaching home, they went into the kitchen, where Papa had set the table with paper plates and take-out pizza, breadsticks, and wings from town. They ate at the table, as Rose told Papa about their day. After dinner, Grama pulled out the cookies from the basket and brought them to the table. Then she pulled the gallon of milk from the fridge, and filled four of her antique glasses. Tonight, Papa got the green glass, Rose got the one with red hearts all over it, Olivia grabbed the plain striped one for herself, and then she slid the flowered one to Grama. Grama smiled at her, knowing Olivia thought the flowered one was the prettiest.

After dinner, Papa went to the living room and turned the television on just in time to catch the end of his favorite program, the nightly news. Once it was over, they settled in for the evening, sitting with Grama on the couch and watching a couple family comedies. Olivia was as tired as she could ever remember. She looked over and saw Rose's eyes shutting, then opening, then shutting again, and she knew it was time to close out their day. Olivia looked at Grama and said, "Grama, I think I'd better take Rosie to bed. She's about to go to sleep, and I know you and Papa don't need to be carrying her upstairs." Grama agreed, rubbed Rose on the back, and talked her into climbing the stairs and settling in for the night. Rose had barely finished brushing her teeth before she was in bed and out cold.

Olivia's mind was full of the day's stories as she laid down on the bed. She let the day run through her mind several times over, the whole time thinking that her great-grandma would be so happy with all she had learned over the course of this day. She knew Great Grandma Baker wouldn't mind her skipping just one night of the pink flowered box, as she just couldn't keep her eyes open anymore after the excitement of the day. The thought had no more than crossed her mind before she drifted off to sleep. The moon was full and shining on Olivia's face, just as it had shone on her Great Grandma Edie's face in the same little town, so far back in time. As Olivia slept, she dreamt of her friends and the joys of spending this time with them. Then, as she fell off into deeper sleep, she dreamt of the children that once played in the same streets, so many years ago.

Chapter Thirteen

A Ride with Papa and Rose

OLIVIA woke early, remembering the dreams from the night before. She was excited to see Sunshine and her other friends, and had a little ache in her heart, knowing that her time with them was about to come to an end. She lay on the bed, thinking about their plans to meet at 11:00 as well as their plans for the rest of the day. Lunch at the train, then fishing at the river cabins, walking the tracks... She wondered for a moment what Grama Truly would have to pack for lunch, and then her mind slipped back to her first lunch on the train. That seemed like a lifetime ago. She had become so close to her friends in such a short time, and she was sad to think she would go back to her country home in Tulip, not knowing how often she would get to come and visit her friends in the months to come. She worried that they might forget how close they had become, and that the friendships would fade over time. She shook off the urge to cry, and decided she'd better make the best of her day. She smiled and said a short prayer, thanking God for the friends he had given her, and added a small request to keep them close forever.

As she slowly crawled out of bed, Rose woke up. Olivia laid with her for a minute, then they decided to see if Grama Truly and Papa were up yet. As they walked down the steps to the main floor of the house, they saw Grama and Papa hugging in the kitchen. They laughed as Grama saw them and waved them over to join in on the hug. They all embraced each other in a giant hug, then Papa picked Rose up and sat her down at the table. Olivia helped Grama carry the bacon and homemade waffles to the table, and Grama carried a little white pitcher full of warm homemade syrup. They sat down, ate, and talked about how much fun the week had been.

Just as they were finishing up, the phone rang. Rose laughed with excitement, knowing who must be calling, and Papa said, "Rosie, you'd better answer that, I think it's for you!" She ran to the living room, picked up the cordless phone, and chattered for several minutes before letting Olivia have a turn. After Olivia talked for a few minutes, she handed the phone to Grama, and Dawn filled her in about what time they would be home on Saturday morning. Grama told Dawn how much fun they had over the week, and what a joy the girls had been. Olivia heard Grama say, "We love you too," then both girls shouted, "We love you, Momma and Daddy!" Grama put them on speaker phone, and let them say their goodbyes, then she hung up the phone.

Olivia and Rose hugged for a minute and talked about how soon Mom and Dad would be home, then they helped clear the breakfast dishes from the table. Rose pulled a chair up to the sink and washed the dishes, while Grama helped Olivia make and pack her lunch for the day. Grama said, "This is a special day for you, Olivia, so let's make sandwiches on these cute mini buns. Then we can put together a small bowl of mixed fruits with some fruit dip, and you can take some of your favorite chips."

After preparing all the food, they packed it all into Grama's picnic basket. Grama said, "I also bought you some special plates, napkins, straws and cups to use, and I made lemonade to taste like lemon shake-ups for you." At this, she winked at Olivia, knowing how much she loved the super-sweet lemon shake-ups from the fair. Grama added that Papa had packed the sandwiches and the fruit in the cooler, so the food would stay cold until they were ready to eat. Olivia hugged her and said, "You two think of everything! But how am I going to get all this to the train?" Grama laughed and said, "I thought about that. Papa is going to drive it down there for you. When you're done, put everything outside the train together, and he will pick it up later. Now, hurry out to the garage, because Papa is getting a fishing pole fixed up for you."

Olivia smiled, gave her one more hug, then asked Rose to come to the garage and spend some time with her before she had to leave. They dressed, put on their shoes, and went to the garage, where Papa had a pole and a small tackle box all fixed up. Olivia said, "Papa, I have no idea how to use the pole, bait the hook, or anything!" Papa laughed and said, "Honey, that's what all those boys are for. Surely they can bait the hook for you and teach you how to cast the line." Olivia laughed, knowing full well that Papa was right about that.

Grama Truly came out of the back door, arms loaded with the basket and jug of lemonade, and Olivia rushed to help her pack it in Papa's old truck. Then he loaded the cooler and Olivia's bike, telling her there was no point in her having to ride there, since he was going anyway. Rose jumped in the front seat, slid into the middle, and asked Papa if she could shift the gears as he drove. Olivia real-ized that this week with Grama and Papa had been special for Rose. She laughed, knowing that Rose had evidently helped Papa drive before. She bet Grama had gotten a kick out of watching Papa teach Rose how to shift from one gear to the next. She could only imagine how entertaining that must have been.

They took off slowly, and Rose shifted through each gear, knowing to watch Papa's foot on the clutch and move it just at the right time. Olivia said, "My goodness, Rose! You and Papa drive really well together!" Rose let out with a loud, excited giggle, as they were headed full speed down Main Street. Then, as Papa reached Second Street, he slowed down and helped Rose shift down to the lower gear. She laughed again, as they coasted slowly down the street until they reached the train.

Papa pulled over, got out of the truck, and stood looking at the train as if he had seen it a million times through the years. He said, "I can't believe this old train is still here, and the paint doesn't look too bad after all this time." Olivia wondered how she had been to visit Grama and Papa time after time, and never once saw the train until this visit. Then she laughed, shook her head, and thought, "I just need to get out more."

As they finished unpacking the truck, Olivia saw Sunshine and her friends walking towards them from Honeysuckle Lane. Sunshine was walking a puppy on a leash, and Ray was walking alongside them. Sunshine said, "Buckeye! I think you should name him Buckeye. He's brown with a small tan spot, right on the top of his head, just like a buckeye." Ray laughed and said, "Okay, Buckeye it is!" Olivia and Rose ran to the puppy, as Olivia asked, "Where on earth did this guy come from?" Rose sat on the ground to play with him, and Olivia sat next to her. Papa told them they had a nice looking pup there, and bent down on one knee to pet him and get a closer look. Ray explained his neighbor's dog had puppies, and now that the pups were old enough to leave their momma, they gave him the first choice of the litter.

Olivia introduced her papa to them one by one, then introduced the boys to Rose, since she had already met the girls at the café a few days before. Papa talked with the boys, showed them the fishing pole he had fixed up, and asked them if they could help Olivia out, since she didn't have much experience fishing. Ray said he would be glad to help, and that he had helped his older sisters in the past, since they really didn't like baiting the hooks. One of the other boys laughed, and said they always helped the girls, and they all laughed when he explained how they didn't like to get worm guts on their fingers.

After Papa was sure the boys had it all under control, he walked with Rose to his truck and told Olivia to check in every couple hours so Grama wouldn't worry. Olivia agreed and ran to give Papa and Rose a hug before they climbed in the truck. All the girls followed, gave Rose a hug, and told her they would see her tomorrow night at the movies. Rose's eyes lit up, and Olivia was glad they made Rose feel important. They watched and waved until Papa and Rose drove the truck away and out of sight.

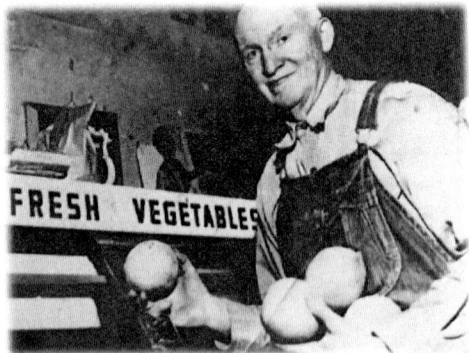

Chapter Fourteen

The Best Friend I Ever Had

THE kids walked along, carrying the cooler and food to the train, as Olivia explained how excited she was to spend the day with them. She stopped, looked at each one of them, and said, "I'm excited, but I'm also sad today, knowing this is my last day to spend with you alone, before I have to go home. I'll see you tomorrow evening for the movie, but Scott, Lacey and Rose will be with me. I've never had friends like you, and I'm afraid you'll forget how close we are, since I won't see you everyday." She started to cry, and they all gathered around and hugged her, promising to never let their friendship be forgotten. After a few minutes, Olivia wiped the tears away, let out with a giggle, and thanked them all for being such great friends. Almost immediately, the mood shifted back to excitement, and they began talking about what the day had in store.

They decided to fish for a while before eating lunch, so they walked to the tree where the fishing gear was and gathered their poles and tackle boxes. Once they had everything they needed, they headed toward Honeysuckle Lane, which led to the river.

Sunshine hung back with Olivia, as they watched their friends stroll ahead of them. Sunshine quietly said, "Olivia, I think you're the best friend I've ever had." Olivia stopped, looked at Sunshine, and wondered if anyone had ever noticed how beautiful she was, not only on the outside, but on the inside too. Sunshine's eyes were glowing, her soft light brown curls draped around her face, and her way out-of-style overalls somehow looked like a stylish new fad, rolled up just below her knees. Olivia hugged her and said, "I feel like we're soul sisters," and at that moment, they both promised to never forget each other. After a quiet minute, Sunshine told her not to worry, and that she would always be there. They gave each other a pinky promise, then with a laugh, ran toward Honeysuckle Lane and the rest of the gang. Olivia somehow knew that today was going to be a day that memories would be made to last forever.

The day went by equally as fast as every other day the friends had shared the whole week. They caught a mess of fish, and the boys cleaned them, as the girls went back to the train, washed the tables, and set the food out to have their last meal of the week together. They ate, laughed, shared stories, and talked about the next night that was planned.

They walked the whole town, went to the sandbar, walked the railroad tracks, and repeated everything they had done the whole week. Finally, at around 4:00, they decided they had better head home. They stood in a circle and just looked at each other in complete silence, for what seemed to be an eternity. Then, slowly, they had a group hug. As they started to go their separate ways, each boy hugged Olivia. Bill, then Will, then Ray. Then the girls gathered around her, Hilda hugging her first, then Erma, then Farol. Last, Sunshine stepped forward. As tears streamed down her face, she said, "Olivia, you will always be our friend. We love you so much." Olivia couldn't even answer back, but they knew. As they all walked away, Olivia walked to the end of the street, then turned back and watched her friends walk out of sight. She turned toward her grandparents' home, then sat down on the street bench and cried until she had no more tears.

When she arrived back at the house, Olivia went inside. Grama Truly knew, before she even saw Olivia's face. She went straight to her and hugged her for the longest time. She told Olivia not to be sad, and that she could visit any time and see her new friends often. Olivia knew Grama was right, and she couldn't quite explain why she was so sad. Rose came over, joined in on the hug, and told Olivia that she would make sure she didn't forget her new friends. She reminded Olivia that they were her new friends too, pointing out that she especially liked Farol.

Olivia talked for a while, telling them all they had done that day. Then Grama talked the girls into coming to the kitchen to help her make dinner. They made tacos, and Rose helped cut up the tomatoes and lettuce, but she let her grandma cut up the onion, knowing it would make her cry. Olivia laughed, and Rose said, "Have you tried it, Olivia?" Olivia said, "I sure have, and you're exactly right! Makes me cry every time!"

While Truly chopped the onion, Olivia and Rose set the table, then called Papa in from the garage to wash up. They sat at the table, ate, and planned for the next day, when Auntie L, Scott and Lacey would finally be home for the summer. They planned a big dinner for Saturday, including strawberry-rhubarb pies, made especially for Mom and Auntie L. Rose spoke ahead for the big rolling pin, declaring that she had mastered the technique of using it over the past week. Everyone agreed that yes, she was the master of the big rolling pin, and it should, of course, be hers to use.

After dinner, they spent some time with the cats, helped Papa feed the dogs, then closed them all up for the night. After coming in, Rose crawled up on Papa's lap, and they watched the Nightly News. Rose finally joined Grama and Olivia on the couch, and they watched one more show together before the girls made their way upstairs to get ready for bed. By the time they showered, they were both feeling the pull of the evening, so they said their goodnights to Papa and Grama, and Olivia handed Rose her blanket and Fred as they made their way to their room.

Rose crawled into bed, snuggled Fred close, and asked Olivia if she would lay with her for a bit, until she could go to sleep. Olivia had developed a patience for Rose, knowing how brave she had been this whole week, and she was proud that Rose had behaved so well for both Grama and Papa. Olivia planned to tell her mom and dad how good Rose was. She was truly amazed that a five year old could behave so well, while she was surely missing her mom and dad so badly. Olivia turned off the lights and cuddled Rose close, until she fell sound asleep. Then she carefully crawled off the bed, being careful not to wake her sister. She needed some time for herself. She still had things to do.

Once she had slipped out of Rose's bed, Olivia went straight to the pink flowered box. There were only two bundles left. She decided that tomorrow she would tell Scott and Lacey about the previous bundles, then finish the last one together. She rested her hand on the second to last bundle, trying not to peek at the bundle below it. She could feel that the last bundle was something more than just a stack of letters. She could feel material, like a sweater, or yarn, so she had to fight the urge to pick it up. She eventually convinced herself that she was too tired, so she wouldn't be able to get through both bundles anyway.

As she loosened the ribbon from the second to last bundle, she saw several newspapers, along with clippings from newspaper articles. The clippings were from life events of Great-Grandma's many grandkids. 4-H events, school plays, where they had made honor rolls at school, graduation pictures, and even engagement pictures when some had become adults.

Olivia noticed the papers began to be more yellow, deeper into the stack. She came across many papers, and she realized the label attached to each one had Raymond Baker's name and address. These were dated in the 1960's, and Olivia realized that her great grandpa had probably read every word on these pages. There was nothing Olivia noticed that would have made her great-grandma keep these, other than the fact that they were delivered to her late husband, and she just couldn't bare to throw them away. The fact that his name was on them made them of value to the woman who had devoted her life to him.

Below these papers was yet an older paper, dated April 2nd, 1955. As Olivia opened it, she realized it was the original picture she had seen of her Great-Great-Grandad Aurthur, in his store. The article said he had been in business over twenty years, which meant that Aurthur's General Store had been in Newberry back as far as 1935. Olivia knew this was a stamp of history, and it excited her to know what years the family had left their mark in this small Greene County town.

As Olivia reached the last few pieces of the stack, she realized again how important family roots were to her great-grandma. Olivia read scribbled notes Great-Grandma had written. Names of ancestors, states where they had lived, and even a note to herself, to visit the Gaston County courthouse in North Carolina, and to ask for ship logs. Olivia knew that she obviously didn't get that far in her journey, and had maybe left these notes for the next generation to take the journey for her. Olivia was excited that she could fulfill Grandma Baker's wishes, do the research, and find out where her family had originated. She knew, of course, that there were many roots to research. Each grandparent had roots, making the many branches that formed this into one of the biggest family trees anyone could imagine.

Olivia wondered what countries all her ancestors had known. She knew, from what her Grama Truly had told her, that she was part Irish and Scottish on Grandma Arthur's side. The notes mentioned that Grandma Arthur's maiden name was Hart, so Olivia decided to start with the Hart side. At that moment, Olivia started what her

Grandma Truly called a bucket list. That would be first on her list as an adult, to visit North Carolina, and ask for the ship logs on file in the Gaston County courthouse. There, she would look for the name Hart.

As the last note was read, Olivia sat by the pink flowered box, and packed the bundles back into the box, feeling the material in the last bundle that laid below the one she had just explored. She knew that tomorrow, she would go through the last bundle with Scott and Lacey, but what she didn't know was what information that bundle held. As she placed the lid back on the box, she whispered a promise to Grandma Edie that she would someday make that trip to explore the ship records.

Olivia put the box back in place and tucked herself in for a good night's sleep. Then she dreamt of the woman whose memories had filled the pink flowered box, and all the ones whose lives she had touched. The moon beams shined through the window, past the window seat, across Rose's bed, and onto the girl that had grown and changed in so many ways over the past week. Scott and Lacey would be here tomorrow, and they would hear all about Olivia's journey this past week. They each had a journey of their own to tell. And again, Heaven smiled.

Chapter Fifteen

The Pink Flowered Box

AS Rose lay in bed, still sound asleep, Olivia quietly tidied their room and organized things in their closet, knowing that Scott and Lacey would be coming within a couple of hours. She couldn't wait to get some time alone with them to share what she had found in the pink flowered box. Olivia was hoping they would be as excited as she was about the history kept inside the box, and she was really hoping the last bundle would be the best of all the bundles so far. Her gut told her this bundle would be special, because she could tell that it was more than just letters this time. She also knew that Great Grandma Edie would not disappoint.

Rose woke up, just as Olivia had finished cleaning. She rolled off onto the floor, and giggled, knowing that Scott and Lacey would be there soon. They could hear Papa moving around in the kitchen, as he listened to his favorite country music station on the radio. As they walked downstairs, they could hear Grama Truly singing along to "You are my Sunshine." Then Olivia recalled her grandma telling the story. She had told the girls that this song was her first memory as a young child. As her story goes, Truly's dad took her to the kitchen early one morning, while everyone in the house was still sleeping. He sat her in a high chair and turned the radio on. This same song had come on and he started to sing it to her. Grama ended the story by saying, "I can still see him smiling at me as he sang."

Olivia walked into the kitchen while Grama was still singing, and she joined in. As their eyes met, they sang like no one was watching. They both seemed to know that their minds were in the same place, thinking of the memory that Grama Truly had shared. Rose went to sit with

Papa at the table, and they giggled as Grama and Olivia continued singing to the tops of their voices. When the song was over, Grama and Olivia joined hands and curtsied, as Papa and Rose clapped for their performance.

Grama hugged Olivia, then took her by the hand, to the Magic Microwave to see what was inside for breakfast. Rose and Olivia knew it was Papa again, when they saw the Egg in the Middles, as they called them. It was a favorite of theirs. French toast, with a hole cut in the middle, then an egg fried in the hole. They knew there was enough for Auntie L and her family, and Grama insisted that they go ahead and eat while it was still halfway warm, so they sat down and dug in. They each ate an egg in the middle with syrup and bacon, and enjoyed listening to the conversation as Papa talked about his friend, and how they were planning a fishing trip for the next Sunday.

As Rose finished her last bite, she heard a sound at the door. She took off running as quickly as her legs would take her, knowing who it was. The door opened, and in walked Scott, who looked much older than the boy they had seen on the last visit. His eyes were the clearest blue, and Olivia gasped at the resemblance she could see of her great-great grandad. Rose hugged him right around his waist, but that didn't seem to be enough for Scott. He bent down and picked her up, holding and hugging her for a long time. Lacey came in next, carrying her bag and blanket. She immediately dropped them at the door and ran straight over to hug and dance around with Olivia. They were like two best friends who hadn't seen each other for an eternity. Auntie L hugged Truly tight for a minute, then noticed Papa standing in line, patiently waiting for his turn. After their first hugs had been given, they all took turns, until no one had missed hugging the other.

After everyone settled in, they all went back to the kitchen and enjoyed the never ending conversation. Auntie L, Scott and Lacey enjoyed the long awaited breakfast. Auntie L said, "Papa, I've waited months for your Egg in the Middle! No one makes them quite like you!" He laughed as he started a fresh batch of coffee. Then he turned and gave her a wink, saying, "That magic microwave has surely been good to your momma over the years, hasn't it?" Auntie L just laughed and said, "I haven't found that kind of microwave yet, but I'm still hoping!" They all giggled, gratefully enjoying the precious time together.

After the last crumb of food was gone from the table, Grama started to clear the dishes, and Elise got up to help. She asked Rose if she would help her and Grama make pies in a bit, telling her she had brought some Rhubarb and fresh strawberries from the store in Bloomington on their way home. Rose told her all about how to mix and roll the dough, and she grew more and more excited as Auntie L hung on every word.

Olivia saw this as her opening to take Scott and Lacey upstairs to fill them in on the pink flowered box and its contents. She whispered to Lacey, then grabbed Scott by the arm, as they walked by him, leaving the kitchen and making their way upstairs.

When they reached the bedroom, Olivia began to spill the story, but no sooner than she had started, Scott and Lacey stopped her mid-sentence. Scott glanced at Lacey, and Lacey said, "Scott, you tell her." Scott smiled at Lacey, then looked over at Olivia, and said, "Let's sit down. This may take a minute to explain." They sat on the bed, and Scott began. "Olivia, Lacey and I have already been through the box, each of us at separate times. I went through it about two years ago, when I was here to visit for a week, and Lacey was at horse camp. I saw the box, opened it to see what was inside, and saw the letter from our great-grandma. After I made my way through each bundle that week, I put it back, sticking the letter out of the edge of the box, in hopes that Lacey would find it next. Last year, when I went on a fishing trip with my friend, Lacey came to spend a week here. She found the letter, and when she was finished, she put it right back for you."

Olivia's eyes were centered on him, listening to every word, as he went on with the story. "Tonight, we'll go through the last bundle, after we go to the movie. We'll wait on Rose to go to sleep, then we'll finish. But that's not all we need to tell you. We're actually going to spend the day with you, but you have to spend the day letting us show you some things. You have to promise right now not to ask any questions. For you to fully understand, you're going to have to take it all in. Then when the last bundle is finished, your journey will be complete."

Olivia already had questions, but before she could speak, Lacey stopped her. She placed her fingers over Olivia's lips, and said, "We are so excited to share the last leg of your journey with you. Scott and I didn't have anyone to share ours with, so this is more exciting for us than you can imagine." Olivia was so puzzled, yet intrigued at the same time. Scott said, "Okay girls, it's time to take a trip around town. Let's ask if we can go now."

Chapter Sixteen

A Walk Through Time

THIS time, Olivia didn't go to the garage for her bike. Instead, as Rose and Auntie L rolled away, making pies and pie dough cookies, Olivia, Scott and Lacey Rae crossed Main and began the last day of Olivia's journey together. The town looked different to Olivia this time, and she wanted so badly to ask why, but Lacey kept giving her a look, so she knew not to ask. The town park didn't have the merry-go-round, or the slide, and it seemed like nothing more than just a see-saw, a swing made out of a flat board, and a couple of picnic tables. The church looked newer somehow, and as they walked down a street that Olivia hadn't visited, there was a large brick building. It was Newberry School, and Olivia realized that it was where her great-grandparents had attended school. As she stood there, her eyes filling with tears, she wondered if she was dreaming. Then she turned to Scott and Lacey, and they, too, were crying.

Scott said, "Girls, let's enjoy this, because we may only have one more journey like this. We will hopefully take this journey with Rose in a few years, then we may never get to do this again. Olivia started to talk, but again, they stopped her. Scott stepped up on the school steps, walked to the door, and they walked inside. As they walked the halls, they looked into the classrooms, and took in every item they saw. There were old books, desks that looked different than those they were used to, and pictures that were all black and white. They went on to find the library, which only had a few shelves of books, then walked past an office, and found a small gymnasium that seemed way too small to fit a crowd of people.

After walking through every inch of the school, they stopped in the hallway to look at the pictures. Scott pointed out one picture of the ball team and cheerleaders, and Olivia wondered if it included their great-grandparents. In another picture, she noticed a girl in overalls, and Scott told her that was Great-Grandma Edie. Then he pointed to Raymond, standing in the row behind her. "This is them," he told her, and Olivia looked in amazement, knowing she would have never picked them out in the group. She said, "How do you know for sure this is them?" He reminded her that a lot of questions would be answered when they got back to look through the last bundle tonight. Lacey held Olivia's hand, and they walked through the double doors, down the steps, across the school yard, and on to the last few hours of the journey.

Scott took them back over a street, then headed out of town. As they got to the town's edge, there stood a beautiful white home, with an octagon window close to the top. Olivia said, "This is the same place Grama took Rose and me. She parked at the barn that was here to tell us that her mom lived here as a teenager." Lacey said, "Yes, that's right. This is Great-Grandma Edie's home." Then, almost as though they knew what they were supposed to do, they walked inside. Again, they took in every detail. Looking at the bedroom where Edie laid at night, Olivia knew the moon had lit her face through the octagon window here for thousands of nights. After taking it all in, they made their way back outside. Olivia was sad when they left, knowing it was just a memory from her great-grandmother's past. She knew how lucky she was to get the opportunity to take this journey, so she reached out for Scott and Lacey, held their hands, and hoped that Great-Grandma Edie was watching at this very moment.

As they reached Honeysuckle Lane, Olivia looked to the right, where the large maple tree stood. She noticed it was smaller today, and a large two story home sat neatly behind it, with a new stone wall wrapping the front of the property. She thought back in her mind, remembering that the first time she saw the tree, she thought there must have been a beautiful home here at one time. Now here it was. After admiring its beauty, Olivia's eyes drifted back to the street. Around the corner, she noticed the train where she had spent so much time with her friends this past week. It now looked almost brand new. The woods had not yet grown up around it, and it looked as if it had just pulled in from a long ride across Tulip Trestle. As they walked inside, they sat down for a minute, and she took a deep breath, knowing it might be years from now that she might get one last visit here, at a place that held so much of her heart.

As they left the car, they walked down the street, and she realized the whole town had streets lined with homes that looked newer than they had the day before. Scott and Lacey walked her to where their great-grandpa had lived as a kid, and Lacey stopped in front, asking Olivia to guess who might have lived here. Olivia had no idea, so they finally told her. Olivia stood there a minute, picturing the young man that must have laid his head here each night. They stepped inside, doing the same as they had at Edie's home, then back out to the street.

After taking one last look at the outside of the simple small town home, they crossed back over and walked a few blocks to the old train station. It still looked old, but it was in way better shape than she was used to seeing it. There were train cars outside, on tracks that weren't there before.

Scott led them back to Honeysuckle Lane, and they spent some time at the river cabins, which lined the river one after another. Knowing the distant uncles had spent time there gave them a feeling of connection to the men they never knew, and they enjoyed the feeling of knowing this was a simple and peaceful life.

They walked the tracks until they had gone as far as Olivia and her friends had gone on the days before, then they made their way back to town. They crossed over Main Street, and then headed to the sandbar. Olivia glanced down Mulberry Street and noticed a home on the lot where she knew her great-great-grandparents had lived when they got older. She couldn't believe the home was now there, on the lot, where she only had imagined how it looked before. Scott explained that the grandparents didn't live there yet, saying they were still living at the house on the edge of town. It was so much to take in, but Olivia was starting to understand.

Once at the sandbar, they stood at the smooth, glass-like water, Scott skipping rocks in silence. After what seemed like only a short moment, he suddenly paused and said, "It's getting late. We had better get home and ready for dinner. Remember, Olivia, no questions until we look through the bundle tonight, and don't say anything to anyone, especially Rose. She needs to take this journey when the time comes for her." Olivia made the promise to keep the journey a secret until Rose's time came. Then, they agreed that they would plan it out, so they could all be there on the last day of her journey, so they could all end the journey together. So home they went, without a single word. Olivia was still wondering if she was in a dream, and doubted she would ever really know. But if so, if this really was a dream, she knew she wanted to finish it. She just knew she was about to finish a journey for which she couldn't begin to imagine the ending.

Chapter Seventeen

Walk in the Rain

AT the dinner table that evening, Olivia could barely look up. Her Grama Truly had always told her that her eyes were such a clear blue that she could look all the way into Olivia's soul through her eyes, so Olivia was afraid that if she looked her grandma in the face, she would surely know something extraordinary was happening. She was thankful that Rose was doing all of the talking during the whole meal, keeping the adults busy. She looked at Scott and Lacey, and she could tell they were nervous too. This hour couldn't pass fast enough.

As dinner was slowly coming to an end, Scott asked Papa, Grama, and his mom if the older kids could camp out in the garage tonight. Grama Truly looked at Papa, and he thought for a minute, then said, "Ya know, I think I can clear out a spot for the old air mattress and some sleeping bags." Lacey and Olivia laughed with excitement, and Auntie L chimed in quickly, saying that would free her up to have a campout with Rosie in the living room. Rose cheered with excitement, and asked Auntie L if they could watch movies and eat popcorn. Auntie L quickly answered back, telling her they could stay up all night if she wanted.

Papa gathered with the kids, and they worked to set up the garage for the night. Once they had everything exactly as they wanted it, Grama found them to talk about the plans for the movie. She asked the girls and Scott to make sure Rose felt included and that they kept an eye on her at all times to make sure she was safe. Knowing that they could spend the night in the garage, going through the last bundle without anyone hearing them, they were fine with taking Rose along for the movie. So when 8:30 rolled around, they gathered their blankets, money for snacks, and Rose, then walked down Main street, heading to the Masonic Lodge, where the movie would be shown on the side of the building.

When they arrived, Olivia couldn't believe what she saw. Arthur's General Store was right there, next to the lodge, just like Grama Truly had described on their day out. There were lights on and people shuffling about inside. Olivia turned to Lacey and Scott, and when her eyes met theirs, she could feel a lump in her throat. They both smiled at her, and then shook their heads, as if signaling to her not to ask any questions. Olivia looked down at Rose, and she knew she had to keep the promise she had made. She followed their lead as they laid out their blankets, just in time to notice that Sunshine was just getting there with her friends.

As Olivia rushed over to see them, she hugged Sunshine, and felt her heart beating hard in her chest. Something strange was happening, and she couldn't tell for sure what it was. She tried to shake the feeling, so she quickly hugged Erma and Hilda, then introduced Scott and Lacey to the group. Olivia noticed that Ray wasn't with the boys, so she asked where he was. Hilda whispered, "He asked another girl to the movies, so he may not sit with us tonight." Olivia was confused that he would abandon her and the rest of their friends on her very last night there, but once he arrived, he came over, said hi, and managed to sit close to them, allowing them at least the chance to talk throughout the evening. By this time it was getting dark, and Olivia couldn't see the girl he brought, but she didn't care. She liked the group as it was, and she didn't see the need to include one more person.

Once their blankets were laid out, spots claimed for the movie, Scott suggested they go to the store and get snacks. Olivia's eyes grew as Scott took her hand and pulled her up from the blanket. Lacey and Rose quickly followed, and within seconds they were opening the door to go inside. The lighting was dim, but Olivia still saw the twinkling eyes of the man at the counter. She realized immediately that he was a younger version of her Great-Great-Grandad Arthur. His eyes quickly met hers, and he walked over, bent down, and hugged her. She trembled inside, but hugged him back, knowing this must surely be a dream. It had to be. He pulled away, looked in her eyes, then spoke. He said, "Olivia, I've heard so much about you from Sunshine, and I'm so glad to meet you." As they released their embrace, he brought them over to meet his wife, who was sitting next to the counter. Olivia immediately fell into her open arms, knowing she may never get this hug again. Her great-great-grandma hugged her back, and she could feel the love radiate into her soul. Olivia prayed that she would remember this moment for the rest of her life.

After the hug was over, Olivia turned around to see Grandad Arthur was giving Scott, Lacey, and Rose some cookies from the glass case at the counter. Before going into the store, Scott and Lacey had wondered if he would remember them, so they were relieved when their eyes met, and they saw the familiar wink and twinkle in his eyes, welcoming them back. He now picked up Rose and put her on the counter, telling her to pick out whatever she wanted. When she cackled with excitement, he let out a great laugh himself. Just then, the door opened, and Sunshine walked in. It was at that moment that Olivia began to realize that there must be more to this story that she still had to learn.

Sunshine talked to Olivia's great-great-grandparents for a moment, then grabbed Olivia by the hand, and said, "We'd better get back outside. The movie should be starting soon." Olivia didn't want to leave, but she knew the choice wasn't hers. She couldn't fight the urge, so she quickly walked back to the counter and hugged them again, telling them she was so happy to have the opportunity to meet them. They returned the hug, and said they hoped to see her again someday. Olivia walked away, thankful, knowing that she had a smaller sibling who would someday take the journey, making it possible for all of them to meet one more time.

When they made their way back to their blankets, Olivia sat down in her spot, and Rose snuggled up close. Olivia snuggled back, fighting the urge to cry. Her friends were talking and laughing with Scott and Lacey, so she joined in on the conversation. She knew she might not see them again for a while, and she didn't want to ruin the last evening with them, so she welcomed the distraction of their conversation and laughter, which actually served two purposes in the moment - allowing her to soak in every last available bit of time with her friends, and keeping herself from crying.

As the movie began, the crowd became quiet, captivated by the pictures on the screen. Olivia sat there, wondering what to think. Did everyone around her see the store filled with customers? Was the crowd of people from the past, or were they from her time? Were they aware of what was going on around them? Scott and Lacey watched Olivia, studying her face, and wondering what she was thinking. They knew how they felt on their journey, so they tried to let her know they were there with her and that all was okay. Their eyes met on and off during the movie, and then it was over.

When it was time to leave, they folded their blankets and walked across Main Street with the group of kids that Olivia had grown to love. Ray walked ahead with the unknown girl, and you could tell that Sunshine was a little sad that he had abandoned them. As they walked down a few streets, it began to lightly rain. Sunshine said, "I need to run ahead! I have new shoes, and I don't want to ruin them!" They quickly hugged and said their goodbyes.

Olivia walked in the rain with Scott, Lacey, and Rose, and as the others said their goodbyes, Olivia watched as they walked toward their own homes, and out of her life. Olivia paused as she saw Sunshine walk into the church entry. At that moment, Olivia stopped and looked back, realizing that Scott, Lacey and Rose had already stopped walking behind her. She stood there for what seemed like a few minutes, trying to figure out what was happening in front of her. Then there it was.

Ray had walked the other girl home, seeing Sunshine in the entry of the church along his way. Soon, he was walking back, stopping to see Sunshine at the church entry. Just a couple of minutes passed as Olivia looked on from a distance, watching everything unfold. Sunshine and Ray came out of the church together, and he bent down, letting her climb onto his back. He took off, Sunshine on his back, carrying her all the way to her home at the edge of town.

With a mixture of rain and tears rolling down her face, Olivia saw the story of her great grandparents unfold before her eyes. The rain stopped, as she looked up at the heavens. That moment had frozen in time, and she knew that her Great-Grandma Edie was smiling down on her right then.

Olivia didn't say a word as she looked at Scott and Lacey. They gave each other understanding smiles, and Olivia grabbed Rose's hand, knowing she would some day understand what she just saw. Scott could see Rose was tired, so he walked to her, bent down, and let her climb onto his back to ride the last few blocks home. Olivia and Lacey wiped tears from their eyes, and whispered to each other. Knowing that Scott was very much like his Great-Grandpa Baker made their hearts smile.

Chapter Eighteen

My One True Love

ROSE was soon sound asleep in the living room, with Auntie L right next to her. Scott, Lacey, and Olivia were gathered in the garage, as Lacey pulled the last bundle out of her bag. She had taken it from the pink flowered box just before the movie, so it would be there and ready for them to open when they returned home for the night. The lights in the house went out, and the ribbon on the bundle was removed.

Scott and Lacey reminded Olivia not to ask questions just yet. Then Lacey explained, "We know you've already figured a few things out by now, but this last bundle holds confirmation of what you probably already know." Scott pulled out an autograph book, and handed it to Olivia. She opened the pages one by one. The first page held the name of the owner, Edith M. Arthur, and was dated Class of 1935-1936. The next pages were filled with classmates' and teachers' names, along with notes and poems from each. There was also a note from Edie's dad and sister, but most surprisingly, a note from Ray, written backwards.

Lacey pulled out a mirror and said, "You need this to read the note." Olivia held the backwards note to the mirror, and it read:

To my one true Love,
You're my Ray of Sunshine, and I promise unto you
I'll be yours till end of time, and your eyes fade their shade of blue
Till the last star falls down from the sky, and time comes to an end
I'll love you till the day I die, and my ring falls from your hand
Forever yours, Ray

There it was, on paper. Olivia's thoughts were confirmed. Sunshine was a nickname for Edie. She knew when she saw Ray carrying Sunshine, that it had to be from the story her Grama Truly had told. Olivia realized that during this past week, she had been on a journey back in time, and through that experience, she had come to know her great-grandparents. She realized that they had been kids once too, and she also learned that she liked them enough to be best friends.

She was especially excited to see the story, told by Grama Truly, unfold right before her eyes. She was touched and proud to see that very moment, knowing when she saw him carrying Edie to her home, at the edge of town, that they would be boyfriend and girlfriend from that day forward.

The material in the bundle was Ray's basketball team sweater. Scott explained that Ray and his friends were on "The Newberries," as they called themselves, basketball team, and that Edie and her friends were cheerleaders for the team. There was a picture of them as a couple, and he was wearing this very sweater in the picture.

There were several pictures of Ray and Edie as teenagers. Olivia, Lacey, and Scott looked at them one by one, realizing that Edie was often in overalls. Olivia laughed, saying, "I can't believe that I didn't catch on! Sunshine was in overalls every single day, and I saw Great-Grandma in pictures with overalls on, but it just didn't click! I also never realized that Ray could have been short for Raymond." Lacey then reminded Olivia, "You do realize what my middle name is, right?" Olivia's mouth dropped, knowing that Lacey Rae was named after Great-Grandpa Raymond.

As the night came to an end, they stacked up the bundle, and neatly tied the ribbon back in place, knowing the next morning, the box would be repacked, and the letter kept inside, until they knew Rose was old enough to see.

Scott, Lacey, and Olivia slept that night with the garage door open. The clouds disappeared, the stars filled the sky, and the moon shone in to light their faces, so all the heavens could see. Edie and Ray watched them sleep, greatly pleased with the journey their great-grandchildren had taken. They returned to the tracks that night, where they would walk hand in hand until the end of time.

Epilogue

MANY years have passed since this day, the day that Scott, Lacey, and even Rose helped me finish the last day of my journey back in time. As you know, we were all able to take the journey because Scott took it first, then put the letter back for the next one to find. He said he hadn't the heart to cheat the rest of us out of that journey. So, Lacey Rae found it next, and he asked her to do the same. After I found it, I of course put the letter back, and four years later, Rose found it and joined the Pink Flowered Box Club.

We cherish what we learned about our Great-Grandma Edith, along with Great-Grandpa Raymond, and both our maternal and paternal Great-Great Grandparents. We will never truly know ourselves what happened the weeks we each took the journey. But whether it was a dream, or real, we will always cherish that time, for it is a common bond we all share that will never be forgotten.

We cherish what we learned about our roots through this journey. We are still searching out more, and are proud to be part of the family that started from two kids roaming the streets and tracks of a small Greene County town. We have shared the contents of the Pink Flowered Box with the whole family; however, we keep secret our own journeys back in time. After sharing the stories from the box, each of Grama Truly's siblings have shared fond memories and stories with us throughout the years, and we have added those to our own pink flowered boxes, which will someday be shared with more family.

We each have pictures on our refrigerators - pictures of our children, parents, Grama Truly and Papa, along with both sets of great-great grandparents. The twinkle of Great-Great-Grandad Arthur's eyes still shows in the picture, but now, we each see that twinkle in our own children's eyes and appreciate, even more, the beauty before and within us all.

Grama Truly is still full of spunk, and still shares stories with us each time we see her. Visits with her are cherished, as are the stories of her life. Through the years, I see more of Great-Grandma Edie in her, and sometimes, in the quiet of the night, right before I drift off to sleep, I hear that soft familiar, soothing voice...All's well that ends well.

For my family, I want you to know our roots are here. Come look, dream, imagine...and if you're lucky, really lucky, you can find them here by the river's edge, skipping stones, and walking the tracks of Newberry. Of all the things I've learned from this, it's to open the box, dig inside, and never be afraid to take the journey. It will take you places you may never have the opportunity to see again.

All My Love,

Olivia

About the Author

The youngest of nine, Edith Rose Hart was born and raised in South Central Indiana, where she now lives with her husband. They built their home, nestled in the woods among the creek and dogwood trees, where she and her siblings walked as children.

Although she has built a career of over 36 years, her favorite times are spent with visits from her daughters, grandchildren, and family. Home is where she now hears the echoes of laughing grandchildren at the creek bed, mixed in the memories of the familiar voices from so many years past.

Throughout her life, she has practiced the art of pie baking and poetry writing, which she learned from her mom. She also dabbles in painting, music, and anything to nurture her artistic soul. But through the journey of writing her first book, she has realized the joy of the words falling onto paper, almost as if the story was already there.